# Miss Ione D. and the Mayan Marvel

# Miss Ione D and the Mayan Marvel

A Steampunk Adventure

By Vaughn Treude and Arlys-Allegra Holloway

Nakota Publishing © MMXVII

# Miss Ione D. and the Mayan Marvel

Photography by Arlys-Allegra Holloway
Guatemala map by Vaughn Treude

ISBN: 978-0-9882442-4-5 (print edition)

Published by Nakota Publishing
http://nakotapublishing.com

# Dedication

This book is dedicated to the memory of Arlys-Allegra's parents, Arlys Ione Rogers Holloway and Billy Dee Holloway. Their names and personalities provided the inspiration for the character of Ione D. Arlys and Billy were an old-fashioned Christian couple who raised six children. They were kind, humble, and generous to a fault, in love with life, learning and the outdoors.

Other works by Vaughn Treude:

Centrifugal Force (2012)

Fidelio's Automata (2015)

# Acknowledgments

We would like to thank the following people:

Our friends and fellow writers of Nexus, for their critiques, feedback and motivation

"Silvermoon" on Fiverr.com for proofreading and editing

Arlys Angelique Endres, for posing for the cover and publicity photos.

Ben Gill, for illustrations for chapters 1-5, 7-9, and 11.

Kyle Dunbar, for illustration for chapter 6.

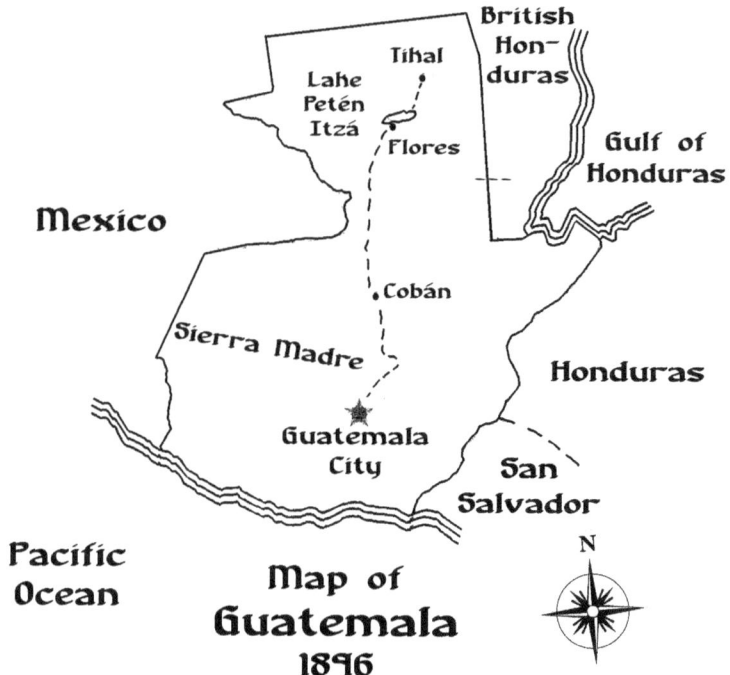

Mexico

British Hon-duras

Tihal

Lahe
Petén
Itzá

Flores

Gulf of
Honduras

Cobán

Sierra Madre

Honduras

Guatemala
City

San
Salvador

N

Pacific
Ocean

Map of
**Guatemala**
**1896**

Showing Ione's journey from Guatemala City
to the ancient Mayan ruins of Tihal.

CONTENTS

------------

**A near miss on a muddy street.**

# I. Disappointment

Muddy water splashed under the wheels of our Benson Electric as the rain poured out of the tropical sky. The clouds were as dark as my mood. Father's transfer to Central America had held the promise of adventure, but so far I'd spent much of my time in the embassy, with its meager library and few opportunities to socialize with those of my own age.

"But Daddy," I said, trying not to sound like a spoiled little girl, "You promised we would go."

"I know, my little cabbage. And I'm very sorry to break my promise, but this is a matter of great importance. As deputy to the Ambassador I must assist in the negotiations between Guatemala and its neighbors. The last thing these people need is war, especially over a petty border dispute."

"Oh drat!" I grumbled. "Men and their stupid wars! We women should have the chance to run things for a while."

"It would be worth a try," Father chuckled. "I doubt that you ladies would do any worse than what we men have done. But unfortunately, even in these enlightened times, people still quarrel with one another, and we must accept that fact."

I nodded. "I understand. I apologize for acting... inappropriately. I would not want you to neglect your duties, especially when peoples' lives are at stake."

"I knew you'd understand," he said, casting me his always-charming smile. "Besides, there is no railway to the north of the country. It's a three-day journey from here to Tikal, and it will be much more pleasant once the rainy season ends."

"That won't be until November," I complained. "The rain doesn't bother me in the least. I would rather be soaked than bored."

"Doesn't your mother take you shopping, and to the theater?"

"Yes. And I love spending time with Mama, but I also crave adventure. Reading about the amazing ruins and the artifacts is not the same as seeing them with my own eyes."

"I'll see what I can do." Father turned his attention back to the road and, seeing a donkey-drawn cart in our path, slammed on the brakes.

"Goodness, Daddy! We almost hit them!"

"And yet he doesn't seem to notice," Father muttered. He tapped the horn several times, until the driver shifted his path to the right, allowing us to pass.

"They should make a rule, for carts and such to remain on the right," I said. "After all, it's almost the twentieth century. Soon, just about everybody will have automobiles."

"I agree," Father said. "But Guatemala is a poor country. Most of the streets are barely wide enough for people to pass both ways, much less have a separate lane of traffic. Still, it is a good idea."

Mother greeted us at the door of our residence, which was located within the embassy gates. She looked impeccable in a lacy lavender dress, her long blond hair tied in a matching ribbon. After she had kissed us both, she said, "Thank goodness you've returned. You are two hours late for dinner. I was preparing to send a search party."

"You worry too much, *ma cherie*," Father said. You know how your daughter is. I could barely tear her away from the University. She bombarded poor Professor Morales with hundreds of questions on the history of this place."

Mother's laugh was like the peal of a silver bell. "*Mon lapin*, I do not understand your fascination with the long-dead past. Nevertheless, I am very proud of you, with your brilliant mind and your thirst for knowledge."

"I only wish they would allow me to enroll in the University here," I said. "It is not fair to reserve the best schools for men only. In England, at least there are women's colleges with proper science programs. I haven't seen one here that has an archeology program."

"You could have remained in London to finish your degree," Mother said. "But I am glad you didn't, because I would have missed you terribly. Come along, you two, let us eat."

We followed her into the kitchen, where our dinner sat warming on top of the coal-fired stove, covered with metal lids. I noted that she had made one of my favorites, chicken cordon bleu. One trait I share with my mother is her love of cooking and the culinary arts. At Father's level in the civil service, we could have had our own cook, but Mother would have none of that. It amazed me that, even here in Guatemala, she could still procure the essential elements of French cuisine.

"I would have missed you, too," Father said with a wink. "But you are a young lady now. Soon you will have your own career, home and family. It is fortunate you began college at sixteen; even with this delay, you will still graduate well before most of your age group."

"Have you heard from the Farrington boy?" Mother asked as we sat down. "He so adores you."

"I received a letter from him just yesterday." Nigel was a sweet boy, and we had attended numerous social functions together, but I did not share his romantic interest. I knew that Mother would be disappointed that I had lost my chance to marry into England's aristocracy, but I believe Father was secretly relieved. He had hopes for me beyond the convention of marriage and family.

Evening approached, and the rains stopped. I sat on the porch reading in the light of the setting sun. The porch was enclosed in netting to keep out the mosquitoes, so I could wear a light summer dress appropriate to the season.

As I savored the scent of the cool humid air, I reflected on my life and regretted that I had been short with Father. For a woman my age, I had seen many wonders. I'd spent my early childhood in Paris, an American citizen by virtue of my birth in the Embassy. My parents had, on occasion, allowed me to accompany them on official functions, where I'd met kings and queens, nobles and aristocrats. Mother had been a celebrated actress until her marriage to Father, so I had also become acquainted with famous actors, actresses and singers.

Shortly after my tenth birthday, my father's job took us to London, allowing me to see the sights and experience the culture of England. There I attended Lady Worcester's School for Girls, where I made many dear friends, some with whom I still correspond. My biggest thrill was accompanying Father on a trip to Egypt, where I saw the Sphinx and the Pyramids first-hand. It was there my interest in archeology was born.

To some people, Father's subsequent assignment to Central America might have seemed like a hardship. In truth, it was his chance to achieve a long-awaited promotion. I saw it as an opportunity to experience yet another land. Ironically, I had not yet visited my own country of America, but Father had promised me that we would go there soon. I was entertaining the thought of finishing my higher education there, though I knew I would miss my parents dearly.

Just as I had returned to my book, the door opened and Father emerged, his after-dinner cigar in hand. "Good evening, little cabbage," he said. "What are you reading?"

"A history of the Maya." I held up the book for him to see. "I am so looking forward to seeing the great pyramid at Tikal."

"You may get that chance sooner than you expect," Father said. You remember Señora Magdalena Ruiz from the embassy office?"

"The translator?" Magdalena was a tiny Mayan woman with the black hair, brown skin and prominent nose of her people. I'd met her at the gala the embassy had held for our arrival. She was fluent in English, Spanish and Mayan, the latter which predominated in the north of the country. I believed she was a widow, but that was the sum of my knowledge about her.

"She hails from a village near Tikal. Later this week she will be traveling there for some family business. I requested that she take you along, and she agreed."

"Really? Oh, Father, thank you so much!" I embraced him, nearly knocking the cigar from his hand. I brushed the ashes from his tie and sat down, trying to calm myself. "What will Mother have to say about this?"

"She won't like it, that's for certain," he said. "But she knows that Señora Ruiz is a practical and competent woman. With her stern demeanor, she could scare away the most ruthless bandit gang."

"Oh, Daddy, you're terrible!" I laughed. "But I will take my hunting knife, just in case."

"Good. Furthermore, the government has stationed a detachment of the Army at the archaeological site, to deter looters and treasure hunters. The President himself has granted you special permission to explore the ruins as part of the U.S. mission here." He fixed me with his gray Welsh eyes. "I promised them you will treat their heritage with the utmost respect."

"Of course. All I wish to gain is knowledge. I will take notes, make sketches, and take many photographs."

"Excellent," Father said. "However, you must be careful, as the jungle can be quite dangerous. You are our only child, and we could not bear to lose you."

I got up and kissed him on the cheek, feeling the roughness of his well-trimmed beard. Father is quite tall, and I had to stand on my tip-toes. "Daddy, I am nineteen years old. You have taught me how to ride, shoot, fence, and fish. You have nothing to worry about."

That night, I lay awake for some time, my mind swimming with excitement over my upcoming journey. After I finally fell asleep, I dreamed that I was exploring the passages deep inside a pyramid when an earthquake buried me alive. I laughed at my own silliness when I awoke safe in bed.

*Miss Ione D. and the Mayan Marvel*

We encounter difficulty on the road.

## II. Departure

On the morning of our departure, I dressed in my favorite riding outfit with breeches instead of a skirt, and tall ostrich skin boots. I'd fixed my long dark hair in a braid that ran down my back. Father brought my bags around to the front of our residence while I went to fetch my horse, Gavilán. As I walked him to the front, I saw a steam-powered carriage come chugging along the cobblestone street.

"Señora Ruiz!" I exclaimed.

"What a surprise! I didn't know she owned an automobile," my father said. "Don't worry, dear, I'll take him." He took the reins from me and addressed the translator as she stepped down from her vehicle. "Señora Ruiz, you remember my daughter Ione." It was jarring to hear him say my given name. He normally used silly pet names, translations of Mother's French endearments, to address me.

"Good day, Mr. Dfrdwy, Miss Ione," Her expression was stern as always.

For a moment I stood there with my mouth agape. She had pronounced our surname correctly as "differ-dwee." Its difficult spelling intimidated most people, which is probably why so many Welsh people went by English names. Our compromise was to use the initial D. "Good day, Señora," I said. "I am most grateful that you've consented to take me along."

"Yes," she said with a nod.

I had forgotten how small she was. I am a petite woman of slender build, and even I was taller than she, by at least two inches. Her festive blue and violet dress contrasted with her sober expression. It was a big change from the gray and black dresses I had seen her wear around the Embassy.

She looked at my horse. "You were expecting to ride to Tikal?"

"Yes, Señora," I said, blushing a bit at my mistake.

"The steam engine is better," she said. No need for rest, only fuel."

I glanced at Father, who gave me a knowing smile. Just then, Mother hurried out to join us, her nose in her handkerchief, sniffling through her tears.

"Take care, *mon chaton*," my mother said as she embraced me.

Though I loved my mother dearly, she could be a bit of a worrier. "Don't worry, Mama. I will be careful, and Señora Ruiz will be there to advise me."

"Make sure you listen to her then," Father added with a wink. He gave me a hug and a peck on the cheek.

I set my bags into the automobile's rear compartment, one containing my clothes and toiletries. The other, larger one was filled with photographic equipment and archaeological tools. There was no room to spare. I felt Magdalena's stare upon me as I struggled to close the lid. It seemed that she had already found a reason to disapprove.

At that moment a horse-drawn taxi clattered up the street and stopped beside us. "Miss D!" cried Professor Morales from inside the carriage. "I'm so glad I caught you!" He hopped from the taxi and thrust a book into my hands. "I believe this will be informative, and will also help you practice your Spanish."

I read the cover. "*Las Ruinas de Tikal.* This is too generous! How can I repay you?"

"By making good use of it," Morales grinned; he was an awkward little man with a bald head and thick glasses, whose suits always looked threadbare. "Besides, I have read it."

"Well, thank you, and good-bye!" I shook his hand, hugged my parents once again, and climbed into Magdalena's car. With a hiss of steam and a crunch of tires on stone, we were on our way.

It was a rare sunny day for the season, and my eyes watered as we rode through the dry, dusty streets. I retrieved my new goggles from my jacket pocket and slipped them on. Since it was a workday the streets were busy with traffic, mostly drawn by horses or donkeys, with a few people riding bicycles.

As we rode, I attempted to make conversation, partly to practice my Spanish, which I had studied daily since our arrival in Guatemala. "Señora Ruiz, how did you come to study languages? I find that subject most fascinating."

"You would be easier to understand," she responded, "If you spoke your native tongue."

"I beg your pardon," I replied, reluctantly switching to English, "My family speaks French and English, but no Spanish."

"Mine spoke only Mayan," Magdalena said. "When I was orphaned at the age of four, my uncle sent me to a convent. There I learned Spanish."

"Did they intend for you to become a nun?"

She shrugged. "I was a sickly child. They did not expect me to survive."

"What made you decide to leave the convent?"

"The religious life was not for me. Also, I met a boy."

"Was it the same one you married?"

"Yes," she said, a hint of irritation in her voice.

"How romantic! You must have been very much in love!" My remark elicited no response from her.

My next few questions were all met with similarly brief answers. If I had not seen how Magdalena interacted with others when visiting Father's office, I would have worried that she disliked me, but this reticence seemed to be her nature.

Guatemala City was the nation's largest city, but technology had just begun to reach it. There was a horse-drawn streetcar, and the government district boasted electric streetlights. My family had arrived via airship to the newly completed Aerodromo Rafael Carrera. When I had asked Father if we could also travel to Tikal by air, he said that an airship was not available and a balloon not practical. Magdalena, I later learned, did not relish the thought of flying.

After we had left the city and passed through a few quaint villages, we came to a place where civilization appeared to end. The road narrowed to a pair of wheel-tracks, and we descended from the mountains on treacherous paths cut into the cliff-side. To me, high places were more thrilling than frightening, but I noticed that Magdalena's knuckles were white as she gripped the steering wheel.

We descended into a lush tropical valley as the trail followed the river. Chattering birds provided flashes of color in the deep green foliage; I was thrilled to see frolicking monkeys among the branches. "This is beautiful!" I had to shout to be heard over the steady thud of the steam engine.

"Yes," my guide replied. After that, I gave up attempting to converse with her. Instead, I took note of everything around me, especially how the trees and the birds differed from those I was familiar with in England. The landscapes in Guatemala were just as green, but the tropical climate here fostered a veritable explosion of life. At a time like this, I would normally get out my pad and sketch, but the jostling of the car on the rough road would make that impossible.

As we emerged from the lowest part of the valley and began climbing the next slope, a loud hissing made me almost jump out of my seat. I looked over at the instrument panel and saw that the needle on the steam pressure gauge had entered the red zone. The throbbing of the engine fell quiet, and we coasted to a stop. Magdalena grabbed the hand-brake lever and pulled it forward, preventing the car from rolling backward.

Magdalena muttered some Spanish words I had not learned in my lessons. "Curse this terrible luck! We may be delayed for some time, and the next village is many miles away. We do not wish to spend the night here."

"Do not worry about me," I said, trying to remain cheerful at the prospect. "I have been camping before, and I quite enjoyed it."

"This is not England, where people spend the night out of doors for fun. The insects will be bothersome, and there are poisonous snakes and jaguars about." She opened her door and hopped to the ground.

"So I've heard." I got out as well. Magdalena opened the lid of the engine compartment. The hiss of the boiler as it lost steam was like a monstrous snake. "Goodness, is that a leak?"

"It is no leak, just the emergency pressure valve." I watched as she fetched a spanner from her toolbox and unfastened the tubing between the boiler and the drive cylinder. I noted the angle of the sun, and wondered if we would indeed be here for the night. Already I was slapping mosquitoes off my neck and face. They even bit through the fabric of my blouse.

She cursed again as she touched the hot engine, against which her thin driving gloves offered scant protection.

"What seems to be the problem?" I asked.

She sighed and pulled a kerchief from her pocket, then used it to hold up the pipe that had connected the boiler to the cylinder. "This pipe appears to be blocked, probably by mineral deposits, which causes the pressure in the tank to be too high. More importantly, it doesn't allow the steam to reach the piston."

"May I see?" She handed me the metal tube, which by now had cooled. I held it to the sky, and saw that no light shone through. "Do I have your permission to try something?" Magdalena shrugged, which I interpreted as approval.

For my recent birthday, my father had given me a kit of paleontologists' tools, which I had packed in my satchel. It included several glass vials containing chemicals that are intended to help dissolve the rock surrounding delicate fossils.

I donned a pair of leather gloves, and then unscrewed the top of a vial. Holding the pipe in one hand, I dripped the acid into its flanged end. It made a bubbling noise as the mineral deposits dissolved. I rinsed the pipe in a nearby brook until the water ran through unimpeded.

"Try this, Señora," I handed the pipe back to Magdalena. It only took a moment for her to reinstall it, and then reignite the boiler from its pilot light. I verified that the needle on the gauge climbed to operational range, but did not reach the red zone. We got into the vehicle and were on our way.

"It was foolish of me not to verify the condition of the vehicle before leaving. We might have been forced to walk to Tikal." A faint smile crossed her thin lips. "Your solution was most ingenious, Miss Ione."

"Thank you." I smiled, feeling gratified to be useful. *And thank you, Daddy.*

The forest grew darker with the approaching night. Magdalena pulled a knob, which ignited a pair of kerosene lamps mounted at the front of the carriage. Despite their brightness, they unfortunately lit only a small portion of the way before us. My heart almost leapt out of my chest when Magdalena slammed her foot on the brake pedal, stopping the car just short of colliding with a herd of peccary. Finally, we came to a clearing in the forest, where a number of tiny adobe houses with thatched roofs lined both sides of the road.

We disembarked from the carriage and approached one of the dwellings. Magdalena called out in words I didn't recognize. An elderly woman answered the door. "This is Akna, my aunt on my mother's side," Magdalena explained.

Akna led us through the tiny house to a room that was open like a porch; a drape of thin cloth served as protection from the buzzing insects, and two straw mats lay on the floor. I removed my boots and jacket and laid down. I was asleep in moments.

The next morning, our hostess served us breakfast—a bowl of cooked meal, probably maize, flavored with bits of smoked pork. The food was simple but satisfying. "*Gracias. Está muy sabroso,*" I said. Akna looked puzzled; I had not realized she did not speak the language.

Magdalena translated my words, which brought a smile to the woman's wrinkled face.

"This is a charming village," I remarked. Through the window of the tiny house, we could see the villagers hard at work in their fields, and domesticated pigs grazing nearby.

They spoke for a while in Mayan. Of course, I couldn't understand a thing, until I heard Magdalena say the word "automóvil," whereupon both women glanced in my direction.

"I told her how you fixed the steam carriage," Magdalena explained. "She says you are a very clever young woman."

"Thank you. I was fortunate to have the proper tools at hand." I was pleased to have helped, but didn't want to seem immodest. After all, what I had done had not been difficult.

After we had finished our meal, I helped Akna clean up as Magdalena gathered wood for automobile's firebox and filled the steam carriage's water tank. As it had begun raining, I was dreading the ride, until I saw her pull a bag from the car's boot and unfold a tent-like canvas cover over the passenger compartment.

Soon, we were ready to resume our journey.

*Miss Ione D. and the Mayan Marvel*

We rode the barge across Lake Peten Itza.

# III. Discussion

Though the cloth cover obstructed much of my view as a passenger, it also shut out some of the wind noise, allowing us to converse without shouting.

Not long after we had left the village, Magdalena surprised me with a question. "Is it true that your father taught you how to shoot and hunt?"

"Yes. In England, my father took me hunting for dove and partridge. I don't relish killing, and would do so only for sustenance. My mother helped me develop many recipes for wild game."

"Among my people," she replied, "The women work as hard as the men. To us, European ladies are pampered. You seem to be an exception."

I laughed despite myself. "No, Señora. I don't think of myself as exceptional, merely fortunate to have parents who are progressive and encourage my independence."

Magdalena furrowed her brow. "So you agree that most white women are spoiled?"

I shrugged. "Perhaps in the upper classes, but I have seen how hard the cooks and washer-women labored at the embassy in London. Still, there is a difference between working for strangers in the city and living close to the land as your people do. To me, your way of life is a difficult one, but I envy your spirituality, which many of us have lost."

After that, Magdalena seemed to relax in my presence. We began conversing in Spanish, as I had dearly wanted to practice that language. Occasionally she would correct my pronunciation, or suggest a better word choice. Though it was frustrating at times, I was grateful for her help.

I asked about her family, and she told me of her parents, and the difficulties she'd encountered after their death. Her sister had chosen the religious life, but it held no appeal for her. At sixteen, she married a mestizo man, who had later perished in a rock slide. After that heartbreak, she relocated to the capital and went into the service of the U.S. Embassy. I began to understand the reasons behind her stern demeanor.

By midday we had descended from the mountains to the forested lowlands, and our progress was faster. The trail was more distinct, and we encountered people walking or driving donkey-drawn carts. To my delight, Magdalena even let me drive for a while. The steam carriage brought plenty of stares from the locals, perhaps more so that it was being driven by a woman, and a white one at that.

Around sundown we arrived at the great lake of Petén Itzá. Our destination, the town of Flores, lay on an island, so we hired a ferry to take us and the automobile across the water.

"I recall reading about this place in my studies," I said. "Wasn't it once the site of a Mayan city?"

"You are correct, Ione. This island was known as Nojpetén, the capital of the Mayan kingdom of Itza, which fell to the Spanish in 1697."

"How amazing! Would it be possible to visit the ruins, even for a short time?"

Magdalena shook her head. "There are no ruins. They were all destroyed."

"How horrible! Who would do such a thing?"

"There were many wars between the different Mayan cities, so some may have been destroyed at that time. But the pyramids were no doubt demolished by the Spaniards, who didn't give us the choice of whether or not to adopt Christianity. They sought to completely eliminate my peoples' past."

I sighed in exasperation. "Surely the Prince of Peace would not have approved."

The town's only inn had one room available, with a single tiny bed, which the two of us shared. The next day was the final leg of our journey. On our way to breakfast at the inn's dining room, I saw a sign that said 'Telégrafo.' "Does that mean telegraph?" I asked. "I would like to notify my parents of our location and progress." The previous night, I had begun composing a letter, but I realized it would take a considerable time to reach them.

"Certainly." Magdalena spoke with the proprietor in Spanish too rapid for me to follow. "They have the new wireless telegraph," she said. Write your message out, the man will send it."

My message sent, I felt better. As we proceeded to the docks, I reflected that it was unfortunate we would not spend more time in this picturesque town, surrounded as it was by the calm blue waters.

Once again we would travel by water, this time on a barge that was headed across the lake. Magdalena's steam carriage shared the deck with its cargo of goats and chickens. She and I sat in the shaded passenger area at the back. It was nice to be able to relax and sketch the wonderful scenery. Some children approached to see what I was doing, and I took the opportunity to speak to them. One little boy wanted me to draw a picture of his puppy, and though I am no artist, I did the best I could. He was so excited when he showed it to his parents.

We disembarked at the village of San Roman, and found a crude dirt road heading north. The way was so narrow that one car would be forced to the side to let another pass. On the good side, the surface was packed well enough that the rain had not turned it to mud.

We traveled for several hours more, until I saw a block of stone rising above the trees. "There it is!" I cried. "The great temple of Tikal!" I could feel the butterflies in my stomach as we approached. My companion regarded my excitement with a bemused smile. To her, these ancient wonders were just part of the scenery.

Soon we encountered a hut by the road, staffed by two uniformed men bearing rifles. Magdalena disembarked to speak to them, leaving me in the carriage with its engine idling. I saw her show the President's letter, but they seemed unimpressed. She stood there arguing with them for quite some time, and I began to worry. Just as I was about to join her to inquire what the problem was, she returned to the car and we drove on through. I looked back at the soldiers and noticed the expressions of anger on their faces.

"What was the issue?" I asked her.

"They wanted to charge us a 'fee'," she said as we drove away.

"How much did they want? My father gave me some money

which I could have..."

"No! Soldiers of their sort are no better than criminals. If they discover you have money, you are setting yourself up to be robbed, kidnapped, or worse."

"It would have been terrible to come all this way and not be allowed to pass."

"You needn't have worried. I told them that the President knew where we were, and there would be hell to pay if we didn't reach our destination."

I realized then how lucky I was to have Magdalena as a guide. If not for her, I might have made a fatal mistake.

I pushed the worries out of my mind and turned my attention back to our surroundings. "This place is amazing," I said. "The pyramid ahead reminds me of those in Egypt."

"So I have heard," she replied. "I should like to visit Egypt someday."

As we neared the site, the jungle sounds were drowned out by the sounds of clanking and men shouting, though the trees obscured the actual site. We stopped the car by a large military-style tent, next to which were parked several carriages and wagons. "Wait here," Magdalena said as she disembarked and entered the tent. I sat for a few minutes, impatient to get out and see Tikal. Just as I was getting out of the automobile, my escort returned.

"We will leave the steam carriage here," she said. "First we must find Professor Valdez, who is in charge of the site. He will tell us which areas are safe to explore."

"Valdez…" I searched my memory, thinking of the academics I had met during my forays to the National University. "I don't believe I'm familiar with him."

Magdalena shrugged. "All I know is that Major Garcia instructed me to speak with him."

We continued down the path on foot, into a broad clearing, where I saw where the sounds had been coming from. A team of laborers was removing soil from what appeared to be vegetation-covered hills, revealing stone structures underneath. Other young men, many of them shirtless in the tropical heat, dug around the perimeter with spades and shovels. I must admit that my gaze may have lingered upon them a bit too long. When I realized that some of them had ceased their work and were looking our way, I blushed in embarrassment.

"Come along, Miss Ione; do not be distracted," said my chaperon with a smile.

I followed Magdalena across the site, my heart racing. A whole new world had opened before me. The Central Acropolis, as they called it, was mostly uncovered, but a large number of young men were swarming over and around it.

We proceeded past the pyramid-shaped temple to an area where only a few men were working. They were surveying the area with measuring tape and pounding in stakes at regular intervals. "Is this the Northern Acropolis?" I asked her.

"I believe so. As children, we would sometimes play among ancient ruins, but these are larger than anything I remember."

In the midst of the hustle and bustle stood two men who were engaged in discussion as they watched the workmen. The first, who held himself with an air of command, was a stocky little man who wore khaki shorts and a shirt that barely accommodated his round stomach. On his head was a dusty white pith helmet, upon which were mounted a cluster of magnifying lenses, now swung off to one side. His most prominent feature was a handlebar mustache, which was waxed to a fine point on each side.

The second was much younger, and clearly the subordinate, as he was listening while the older man talked. He was tall, fit, and clean-shaven, with olive skin and a fine head of bushy black hair. He wore a long-sleeved shirt, dark pants and a vest. Despite the hot, dusty work proceeding all around him, he looked as if he was ready to attend a dinner party.

"Señor Valdez," said Magdalena as we approached. "May we have a word with you?" By now, I could consistently follow her Spanish, and was beginning to understand others as well.

"What is it?" snapped the portly little man. His eyes fell on me and his expression softened. "I beg your pardon. How may I help you ladies?"

"I am Magdalena Ruiz of the United States Embassy." She extended her hand to shake his, as men do. "This is Miss Ione Dfrdwy, daughter of Deputy Ambassador John Dfrdwy."

"Pleased to meet you, Señora Ruiz, Señorita Diff..."

"D is fine," I said, extending my hand to follow her lead. "Ione D." His handshake was limp and clammy.

"And this is my assistant," Valdez indicated the younger man, "Señor Enrico Batista of Mexico City."

When I offered my hand to Señor Batista, he turned it over and kissed it, then gazed into my eyes. "Your loveliness is surpassed only by your courage in visiting this wild land."

"Thank you," I replied. Though I questioned his flattering words, the intensity of his dark chocolate eyes made me want to believe them.

"Señorita D is a student of archeology," Magdalena explained, "And we have permission to visit the site." She handed him the letter, which he scanned quickly before handing it back. "We are here to ask what areas we may explore."

"Most of the central part of Tikal is safe," Valdez began, "but take care that you do not stray too far into the jungle. There are dangerous predators in the forest."

"I see," I nodded, glad I had my hunting knife concealed in my boot.

"Please avoid the areas where our men are working. I won't allow anything to delay the digging. If either of you gets injured, I will not be held responsible."

"Of course," Magdalena assented.

"As for the temple, the shrine at the top is open, however, there is currently no way to get to the interior. Some of the stones are crumbling, so I ask that you not climb it without a guide."

I started to object, but Magdalena put a hand on my arm.

"Do not be distressed," Batista said. "I would be delighted to offer my services as a guide, if the Professor would grant me a few hours leave."

"We shall see," Valdez said. "But at the moment, Mr. Batista and I have much to discuss."

"Thank you," said Magdalena. "We apologize for the interruption."

As we walked away, I told her, "His worries for my safety are groundless. I had a good look at the pyramid as we passed, and I have climbed many slopes more dangerous than that."

"A bit of caution is preferable to injury, or worse," she replied.

I smiled in response. Though the two women were different in many ways, it was exactly what my mother would have said.

Atop Temple IV, I could see all of Tikal.

# IV. Destination

"I wonder where all the workers stay," I mused.

Magdalena pointed to the west, where protruding from the forest I could see another pyramid, which I remembered was called Temple IV. Between there and the work site was a cleared area where stood a village of tents, smaller versions of the one we had first encountered, arrayed in neat rows. As there did not appear to be any women among them, there was no particular need for privacy.

We, however, would need to make our own campsite. My parents had furnished a tent for Magdalena and myself, a new self-erecting model, which only required one to turn a crank, then pound in a few stakes. We found a nice level area some distance from the main encampment, to the east of the temple complex. As I had said earlier, I had slept outdoors before on family outings, but never under such primitive conditions.

"Now that we have made our camp," I said, "we can finally begin to explore the site."

Magdalena exhaled loudly; she appeared to be weary from the journey. "I would like to rest for a while. Allow me to relax for an hour or so, and then I shall be happy to accompany you."

"That is fine," I said, trying not to express my impatience with the delay.

She spread out her mat inside the tent and lay down. Soon I heard her snoring. I was more than happy to let her sleep, but I would go exploring while she rested. After all, I had not promised to wait for her.

My heart beat excitedly as I considered where to go first. According to Morales' book, Tikal had been abandoned centuries ago, rediscovered in 1848. The Guatemalan government had recently commenced its restoration. Only a small portion had been uncovered. Most of the ruins looked like brush-covered hillocks with crests of stone on top.

I walked around the base of the temple pyramid, seeking the best route to ascend. I approached the front face and began scaling it with slow, deliberate steps, glad I had worn dungarees rather than a skirt. The steps were very steep, with the stones broken and loose in places. Nevertheless, it was not a difficult climb and I increased my pace.

Then, as I neared the halfway point, my left foot slipped, sending a huge chunk of rock bouncing down the irregular slope. I fell to my hands and knees, scraping my palms and hitting my nose on the stones. "Bloody heck!" I cried, but that was not the end of my troubles.

My whole body slid downward so quickly I feared I would tumble to the bottom. Without stopping to think, I thrust my right hand out and grabbed the edge of the stone step, preventing my fall. I lay there for a while, heart pounding, until I got up the nerve to continue. For the rest of the way I proceeded much more slowly.

When I reached the summit, I turned around to survey my accomplishment. The jungle was at least a hundred feet below me. A fall from this height would almost certainly be fatal, but the stones here felt quite secure under my feet. In any case, I have always found high places more thrilling than frightening.

Up here, the air seemed much fresher than in the jungle below, though I could still smell tropical flowers on the breeze. I could see three more pyramids in a rough line moving westward, ending in the one they called Temple IV. All were of comparable size, but still shrouded by dirt and vegetation. How exciting it must have been to see these ancient wonders for the first time!

I turned away from the vista, to the stone edifice behind me. On its roof was an enormous carving of an ancient Mayan king, flanked by serpents and scrolls. Though worn by the weather, it looked far more beautiful than the photographs I'd seen. Facing me was an open doorway leading into a dark chamber. I entered, wishing I hadn't left my explorer's head-lamp in our tent.

The enclosed area was a narrow empty room that smelled of the dust of the ages. As my eyes adjusted to the light, I saw a second door, which led into another chamber. Unlike the plain lintels on the outer door, the beam above was covered with ornate carvings of people, animals, and birds. I wished I had brought my sketch paper and charcoal pencil. By placing the paper on the surface and rubbing the pencil across it, one could easily duplicate these wonderful pictures.

"Ione! Are you up there? Come down at once!"

I exited the shrine and saw Magdalena, appearing tiny at the base of the pyramid.

"The ruins aren't safe!" she cried in English, followed by some Spanish I didn't understand.

"Alright, Señora!" I called to her. "Just one moment!" I knew she meant well, but it was all so unfair. I was nineteen, and she was treating me as a child. Besides, a few minutes more weren't going to make any difference.

As I grumbled to myself, something caught my eye. A tiny blue and white dot floated in the sky over the jungle to the south. I stared at it, puzzled, as it grew larger.

"Look!" I called to Magdalena below and pointed to the sky. "A balloon!"

The teardrop shaped gasbag was dyed in vertical stripes in the colors of the Guatemalan national flag. I was envious of the pilot, of the calm, scenic, and fast trip that he made on weekly intervals. I knew how some people grew tired of their work, having done the same for year after year. I, however, would never do so, not if I could soar like a hawk over the majesty of creation.

That experience would have to wait for another day. I descended the pyramid with my face to the megalith, which seemed the safest way.

Despite my near-mishap, I didn't feel that the pyramid was dangerous. I needed to remember to be more cautious on my next climb. As I made my way down, I imagined the long-dead kings and queens beneath my feet and the treasures they had taken along to the afterworld. The greatest treasures, however, would be the knowledge that would be gained by science.

When I reached the ground, Magdalena was waiting with a scowl on her face. "Good gracious, there is blood on your face! Your father expects me to ensure your safety."

"I'm sorry." I pulled out a kerchief to wipe my face.

Magdalena continued scolding me. "At the very least, you should have told me where you were going."

She was right; I should have at least left a note. Still, it was difficult for me to listen, as I was not the kind to repeat my mistakes. "Again, Señora, I apologize. Over there, do you see? The balloon is landing. Do you know what its purpose might be?"

She looked over her shoulder at the blue and white globe looming over the trees. "I would imagine it is bringing supplies from the capital."

"And would they bring anything back with them?"

"It would stand to reason. If I were Professor Valdez, I would use it to send some of the most important finds back to the university."

"Of course!" I remembered that I still had the letter, which I had completed during our ride on the barge. "Excuse me, Señora, but there is something I must do right away." I hurried along to our tent and found my unfinished letter and pen and ink. I wrote a few quick lines about our arrival in Tikal, and then placed the letter in an envelope, which I had already addressed to my parents, care of the US Embassy.

I was greatly relieved to see that the balloon had net yet departed, and was still visible, looming over the trees. As I ran toward its landing place, I passed Magdalena going in the other direction. "Miss Ione," she scolded, "Must you run everywhere you go?"

I had no time to answer; I had to reach the balloon in time. It was tied down near the tent that served as Major Garcia's headquarters. There I saw a man whom I assumed to be the pilot, a dark-skinned man wearing unseasonably warm clothing and a broad-brimmed hat. He had just finished signing a paper, which he handed to a uniformed man I assumed was the Major. He was a tall, stern looking fellow, and he gave me a disdainful glance before returning to his tent.

A pile of goods from the capital, including sacks of flour and dried beans, had been neatly stacked at one side of the clearing. The balloon's basket had already been re-filled with a number of boxes of and crates of the sort I'd seen at the dig. As the pilot turned to climb into his conveyance, I caught up to him.

"Señor," I said, struggling to catch my breath. "Could you please make sure this letter reaches my father at the United States Embassy?"

He shook his head. "I'm afraid I don't know your father, Señorita."

"Then would you be kind enough to mail it when you get there? I have already affixed postage." Though I had not seen a post office anywhere on our journey, I was glad I had brought the stamps along anyway.

"I'd be happy to do that for you," he said with a bemused smile. "May I ask what finds a young girl like yourself out here in the jungle?"

"An adventure, Señor. An adventure!"

He gave a hearty laugh as he climbed into the balloon. "Well, then I wish you the best."

I watched him as he fired up the burner and rose into the air. When he had disappeared over the tree tops, I turned to go. As exciting as it was to be here, I wished I could be home, just for a moment, to take a nice hot bath.

As I returned to our campsite, I noticed the sun was low in the sky and realized that I was quite hungry. On this journey we had not eaten more than twice a day, still, my stomach rumbled at the approach of supper-time. When I reached the tent, Magdalena said, "Professor Valdez has invited us to join him for dinner. You'll need to wash up and be presentable."

"I would be delighted—to eat as well as bathe."

"Then assist me in carrying these things into the tent."

Next to our tent there were two wooden buckets filled with well water, and a large metal tub. As my chaperone carried the tub, I struggled to bring one of the water buckets inside our tent. I shivered as I sponged myself off with the cold well water.

After cleaning up, I donned my favorite blue dress, one of the few I'd brought with me, and then combed out my hair. Normally I wear it long and straight, but this tropical climate would make that style uncomfortable.

Magdalena chose an attractive native dress in green with red accents. She put her hair up in the braided style favored by the locals. When I admired its beauty, she was kind enough to fashion mine in the same way. I imagined how fetching the style would look on Mama, and promised myself I would show her on my return.

We met the Professor at the mess tent, which was located midway between the main excavation site and the tent that served as army headquarters. All tables were vacant save one. We joined Valdez at that last table, where he sat with two other men, one younger, and one that was near his age.

The Professor and his guests rose to greet us. He was all smiles, with no trace of his earlier gruffness. "*Buenas noches, Señoras. Los dos ustedes ves hermosa esta tarde.*"

I sighed, realizing I would not be able to relax, if the conversation was to be all in Spanish. By now I understood the language fairly well, but to use it still required a mental effort.

"Señores," he continued in Spanish, "This is Señora Ruiz of the United States Embassy and Miss Ione D, daughter of the Deputy

Ambassador. Ladies, this is Baron Oskar von Tuntenhausen of Austria-Hungary, and of course, Señor Batista.

"Good evening, Herr von Tuntenhausen," Magdalena said, approaching the baron to shake his hand.

After they had exchanged pleasantries, I followed suit, though I did not attempt to pronounce the baron's name. "I am pleased to meet you, Excellency."

"Also I am," he replied in English. He was a bear-like man with a bushy beard and a pipe clamped in his teeth. "It is most pleasant to be converse with those of the fair sex out here in the wilderness."

I smiled in response, inwardly cringing at his grammar and pronunciation. I hoped I didn't sound like that when I attempted to speak Spanish.

Batista greeted me in English. "Good evening, Miss D." He gave a short bow. His English was good, though a bit accented. "I hear you have already been exploring the ruins."

"Indeed," I said. "I find Tikal to be most fascinating, and beautiful."

"And now, let us dine," said the Professor. He motioned to the empty seats on either side of his place at the head of the table. He pulled out Magdalena's chair for her while Batista rushed to get mine.

I would not have expected such a fancy dinner here in Tikal. It was more like eating at a luxury hotel, with three young local boys serving as waiters. They even dressed the part, wearing white shirts, black pants, and black neckties.

The menu featured a delicious roasted fowl, local vegetables including beans and yams, and an excellent French wine; I glanced at the label and noted its expensive vintage. Dessert was hot coffee and a delightful caramel pudding from Mexico, which they called 'flan'. I thought of Professor Morales back at the University, who seemed to be unable to afford a new suit, and marveled that his fellow professor could enjoy such amenities in the jungle.

The conversation centered mostly on the university's work in Tikal. "The President of our country has given our work here a high priority," the Professor explained. "He wishes to establish Guatemala as more than an exporter of coffee and bananas, but rather as a bastion of knowledge and culture."

"Our Emperor has a strong interest in the antiquities, and also for the people of Guatemala to assist," the Baron added. His interests were more political, and asked Magdalena and me about the American view on this and that. His Spanish was not good, nor his English. At times the Professor would translate our remarks into German for him.

The Baron was most concerned about the threat of war between Guatemala and its neighbors, and with the Professor's help, he pressed Magdalena for news of the situation. I was interested to hear how she would answer, as I expected that the details of the negotiations would be confidential.

Batista, however, had no interest in their discussion. While the others spoke of these serious matters, he besieged me with questions about my upbringing, education, likes and dislikes. Not wishing to be rude, I answered his queries as briefly as possible. Unlike my English suitor Nigel, he was not awkward around girls.

Professor Valdez spent most of his time listening. He laughed at the Baron's jokes and threw in words of agreement in the right places. He was generous with wine, though I demurred after my second glass.

I was excited to hear about the dig. How many students worked here? Had many artifacts been found? What was the approximate date of these finds? Valdez evaded my questions with vague generalities, much like my responses to Batista.

After we finished our dessert, Magdalena stood, and said, "Thank you, Professor, for a delightful evening. But now, Miss D and I must retire."

I echoed her thanks, and Batista sprang from his seat. "Allow me to escort you ladies to your tent. The jungle can be dangerous."

"Thank you, but I'm sure we can manage," I said.

Batista prevailed, however. He hurried around the table to open the flap of the mess tent for us. As we emerged, it was once again raining.

"One moment, ladies!" Our escort dashed inside to produce an umbrella, which he opened and handed to me so that Magdalena and I could take shelter. It was only a light drizzle, but he walked next to us in the rain as if it was a noble sacrifice.

"What a delightful evening, was it not?" he asked. "So much fine food and drink, I am already feeling sleepy."

"Indeed," I responded. As we went, I looked around carefully, trying to fix in my mind the appearance of our surroundings now that it was dark. This was something I might need to know at some point.

We passed a tent that was much like those of the students, but much larger. In front of it, next to the smoldering remains of a campfire, were several stools of the sort that had fabric seats and folded up for easy transport. I noticed him staring in its direction.

Magdalena must have noticed as well. "Is something the matter, Señor Batista?"

He shrugged. "It is nothing serious. I see that the Professor has once again forgotten to douse his fire. Although the frequent rain minimizes the chances the fire will spread, I shall stop by on my return trip to make sure it is has been extinguished."

"That is most responsible of you," I said.

"Thank you once again, Señor Batista," Magdalena said as we reached our campsite.

"It was my pleasure. And now Señora Ruiz, Señorita D, *buenas noches*." He bowed with a flourish and departed.

An earthquake reveals a hidden structure.

# V. Discovery

After we had changed into our bedclothes, Magdalena remarked, "Miss D, I'd be wary of the young Mexican. He seems to be quite the Don Juan."

"You need not worry about me. Even as a young girl, I was never impressed by flattery. I much prefer intelligence and honesty over charm." I lay staring at the canvas above us, as the rain continued its pitter-patter. "I wonder about the Professor, though. Do you believe he is honest?"

She paused a moment before responding. "What do you mean by that?"

"I was wondering, how does he afford to live so well in such a remote area?"

"Perhaps he has a wealthy sponsor,"

said Magdalena.

"I see." I was not convinced. "And the way they were speaking in German. I realize that the baron has trouble with English, and more so with Spanish, but I found it rather rude."

"So did I," she agreed, "Especially since they were talking about us."

"What? You speak German as well?"

"Yes, although he speaks it with a rather pronounced Austrian accent. Valdez' German is almost as poor as von Tuntenhausen's Spanish, but at least he speaks slowly."

"What were they saying?" I turned to face her and lowered my voice, as if someone might be listening. I hadn't expected to encounter intrigue in this place.

"Valdez was trying to reassure him. The baron wanted to know if we would be trouble."

"Why on earth would he assume that?"

"Maybe he thinks that because we are women, we need to be looked after."

"Or perhaps there could be another reason, that there is something going on which they don't wish outsiders to observe."

"Are you implying the Professor is up to something improper?" She shrugged. "I would not rule out that possibility."

I sighed. "Either way, I do not like it." I tried to put the thought out of my mind and settled down for some much-needed sleep.

I arose at dawn. Magdalena was still asleep, which was unusual for her. Perhaps it was because of the previous night's wine, which I had never before seen her consume. My stomach rumbled as I thought of the hearty breakfasts we had enjoyed on our journey. I grabbed some of the hardtack we had brought with us, washing it down with well water. Then I removed a page from my sketch pad and jotted a note: *I went exploring, will be back soon.*

Once again, I wore my riding breeches and cap, with a light jacket, not for warmth, but to protect my skin from thorns. As I left the campsite, the rain began with a refreshing sprinkle.

I thought first of revisiting Temple I, in hopes of finding an unseen passageway inside, but decided instead to go the other direction. Perhaps I might discover something.

According to the book Morales had given me, Tikal was once a great city, with streets and avenues, many of which remained as trails through the jungle. From the map, I recalled a road that headed southeast, and I soon found a path in that direction. On my way, I paused often to jot notes in my journal, draw sketches of trees or wildlife, and record compass headings.

The buzzing of the insects was as loud as always. Mosquitoes flew around my head, but they didn't bite me, because I had applied essence of citronella to my skin at Magdalena's direction. The trees were alive with colorful birds, and the shrieks of howler monkeys kept me alert. Once, I startled a coatimundi crossing my path. I'd seen these fox-like creatures in the Regent's Park Zoo in London, but never in the wild. I wondered, could they be tamed?

Shortly after scaring the coati, I received a scare of my own. The birds commenced a terrible ruckus, and the earth began to shake. I lost my footing and tumbled to the ground. With a loud crack, a large branch fell inches from my head. The shaking was over in seconds, whereupon I got up and dusted myself off. Looking around me, I saw that nothing seemed to be damaged except a few trees.

Checking my pocket chronometer, I recorded the time of the seismic event in my journal. From my geology class, I knew that one or more aftershocks might follow. When the next tremor came twenty minutes later, I was prepared, and was able to stay on my feet. However, the sound of falling rocks caused me to look around in alarm. With great caution I headed into the woods from whence the sound had come. Twice I was forced to use the knife from my boot to cut vegetation out of the way.

I came upon a hill, which exhibited the telltale pyramid shape. Though it was much shorter than the other temples in Tikal, it had the same kind of stone outcropping on top. Though overgrown with vegetation, it seemed like a miniature version of Temple I. My heart raced with excitement. This site had not been on the map in Morales' book. Had I discovered a structure that had been lost for centuries?

As I approached, I saw a crack had opened in the side of the hill, revealing and in some places splitting the limestone blocks underneath. Inside the chasm was darkness, mysterious and yet inviting.

From my pack I retrieved another birthday gift from my parents, an explorer's pith helmet with a lantern on top. I lit the lamp, put the helmet on, and slipped inside sideways, holding my breath to pass through the narrow opening.

I surveyed the dank, dusty chamber, as my lamp lit up the stones beneath and around me. It was hard to contain my excitement when I realized that I stood upon a landing atop a flight of stairs cut into the rock. I marveled that this passageway was unobstructed after the earthquake. The Mayans must have been skilled architects, to create buildings that would stand for centuries despite the region's seismic activity.

As I descended, the only sound was my breathing. My headlamp cast ghastly shadows upon the stones. I tried not to think of the earthquake that had opened this place, and hoped there would be no further tremors.

After the equivalent of two or three floors, the passageway leveled off. Before me stood a great wooden door, much like the carved lintels in the shrine at Temple I. Along its right edge was a dark line that marked a recess at the edge of the wood. After checking for bugs and spiders, I inserted my fingers and pulled. The door moved, but only a fraction of an inch. My subsequent attempts had no effect. Perhaps with assistance I could open it.

With a sigh, I returned to the surface. Despite my wish to explore, the morning sunlight was a welcome sight. Before heading back to our camp, I placed branches across the gap to conceal the opening.

When I returned to the camp, Magdalena's usually impassive face was red with fury. "Where were you? I cannot fulfill my duty to your parents if you wander off."

"My apologies, Señora Ruiz. I didn't mean to compromise you."

"Please don't do it again. By the way, Mr. Batista stopped here earlier and volunteered to be your guide if you wish to explore any of the temples."

"How unselfish of him," I said with a smirk. He was an attractive fellow, but I did not relish his attentions.

"So," my chaperon continued. "What were you up to? When I awoke and you were not around, naturally I was worried. I spoke to Valdez, who told me no one had seen you."

"I did leave a note," I replied. "Did you not see it?"

"Yes, but you were not specific on where you had gone, nor on when I could expect your return."

"That is difficult to know, when exploring," I smiled, and lowered my voice. "And I have made a very interesting discovery, but I wish to discuss it with you first, before informing anyone else."

She surprised me by smiling. "Very well, we shall discuss it over lunch."

"That sounds delightful." After all the excitement, I was quite famished.

Magdalena brewed coffee and cooked tortillas on the campfire, with roasted vegetables and bacon. I was pleased to see fresh mangoes, as I was becoming weary of our usual fare.

As we ate, I told Magdalena how the earthquake had cracked opened the undiscovered pyramid, and how I had descended the stairs to the door, which was too heavy to move.

Magdalena pondered as she sipped her coffee. "That is an amazing story. Do you think the Professor is unaware of this place?"

"I would assume so. The site was pristine and some distance off the trail."

"And why shouldn't we inform him of your find?"

"As I said last night," I said. "I am not sure he can be trusted. It seems suspicious that he lives in luxury here, so far from civilization. Yet back in the capital, Professor Morales barely earns enough to afford new clothes."

"Are you implying he is illegally selling artifacts?"

"Perhaps. After all, you did say that Guatemala had a problem with corruption."

"True," she nodded. "But you should not make such accusations lightly."

"I'm not. But I intend to watch him carefully."

"Still, Valdez will find this place eventually. What do you propose?"

"I am curious to see what is behind the door. No matter what we discover, I will disturb nothing, just take photographs. Afterwards, we should conceal the opening."

"What would that accomplish?" she asked, pursing her lips.

"I intend to tell Professor Morales first. I want to ensure this find is not exploited. If Professor Valdez is honest, he will understand and blame my youth for this transgression. If not, and if he has been selling antiquities for profit, he will be found out."

Magdalena thought for a moment. "I will consider your proposal, but I also wish to see this place for myself. How long will it take us to get there?"

"Twenty minutes at most." My return trip had been much shorter without stopping to take notes. "Let's hurry, before Batista arrives and insists on accompanying us."

We packed our rucksacks, filled our canteens with water, and were on our way. Magdalena took her sturdy walking stick. Its purpose had puzzled me at first, since she had no difficulty walking, but I realized it could also serve as a cudgel. I was glad we had this, in addition to my knife.

As we walked, I often glanced over my shoulder to see if anyone was following. Though I saw only birds and monkeys, I had the uncomfortable feeling of being watched.

When we reached the site, Magdalena said, "I would have noticed this even before the earthquake. The shape of the pyramid is unmistakable."

"Yes." I slipped on my leather gloves. "Please help me clear the brush away."

Soon we were descending the dark stairs into the earth, with my helmet lamp lighting the way. Magdalena's breathing behind me became loud and ragged.

"Is anything the matter, Señora?"

"I feel that this place holds great power."

We reached the bottom. My light played upon the timbers, showing images of kings, gods, and demons carved into its surface. "Let us try to open it."

Magdalena nodded. The two of us inserted our fingers into the recess I had tried early. Pulling together, we moved it half an inch, but no more.

I sighed. "It seems hopeless."

"It's not like you to give up so easily." My companion cracked one of her rare smiles. We shall try a lever." She pulled the brass fitting off the end of her walking stick, revealing a tapered, blade-like end. This she inserted into the narrow gap at the bottom of the door.

We leaned on the stick with all our strength. From the cracking noises, I thought it might break, but instead the door moved out several inches.

"Yes!" we cried in unison. After we had pried with the staff several more times, the door was open far enough for us to slip inside.

The hairs on my neck stood up as we entered the chamber. It was so quiet, I could hear the hiss of the flame in my headlamp.

The air was dusty, dry, and stale like that in the shrine of Temple I, only more so. I sneezed, ruining the solemnity of the moment.

"*Salud*," said Magdalena as she stared, open-mouthed, at our surroundings. The walls were painted in vivid colors, with images of parakeets, monkeys, and iguanas. Tall clay pots lined the chamber, decorated with elaborate geometric patterns. In the center was stone slab on which sat a large oblong box of the same wood as the door.

"Could that be a coffin?" I asked.

"It certainly looks like one."

"Would you object to opening it?"

"No," Magdalena replied, again surprising me.

Working together, we slid back the heavy lid. I gasped at the sight, and Magdalena crossed herself. Inside lay a body in burial garments. Though the skin had dried and shrunk over the ages, her beauty was still evident. On her forehead was a gorgeous beaded band, surrounded by the remnants of a spectacular feathered headdress. A lovely piece of turquoise shaped like a cockatiel's beak adorned her nose.

"A queen," Magdalena breathed.

Her hands, which were folded across her chest, each held a pair of birdlike figurines of identical shape and different composition. Her left hand held figures of silver and obsidian. In her right were gold and turquoise. All were about three inches long. Most breathtaking was the one at her neck, beneath the trace of a leather necklace, now decayed. It was made of a translucent white crystal, almost milky in appearance.

"Do these represent gods?" I asked. "Or perhaps angels?"

Magdalena shrugged. "I do not recognize them."

"Professor Morales will be quite excited to see these."

"What? Surely you do not intend to remove them from the coffin?"

"Of course not," I said. "This is the reason I brought my camera."

The Queen was beautiful even in death.

# VI. Discord

Magdalena watched as I removed the camera from my rucksack and assembled the tripod. "Do you have enough photographic plates?"

"My camera does not need them. It uses the new flexible 'roll' film. In addition, my father has invented a cylindrical container which is sealed against light. That way I can change film without a darkroom."

"Is there enough light in here?"

"One can photograph practically anything, given sufficient time. Could you hold this," I removed my helmet and handed it to her, "and illuminate each subject?"

I photographed the paintings on each wall, the carvings on the inside of the wooden door, and the royal corpse. I left the shutter open for seconds at a time, and hoped that the tripod was steady enough to prevent any blurring.

The objects on her chest would require special attention. In my bag I had packed another of my father's inventions, a magnifying lens which could be attached to the front of the camera.

Because this lens also magnified the image in the camera's viewfinder, I could see the decorative birds much more closely. "You must see this!" I moved aside to give Magdalena a look. "The figurine at her neck looks like quartz, but also seems to contain hundreds of tiny inclusions."

"How lovely!" she exclaimed as she peered through the viewer. "Like bubbles frozen in glass."

"And priceless." Noticing Magdalena's frown, I added, "Not that they should be sold, of course, because their greatest value is to science."

Magdalena's hand trembled a little as she attempted to hold the lamp steady. "Closer, please," I breathed. "The crystal bird will be difficult to photograph without extra illumination."

As she moved in closer, a beam of light struck it, and it issued a surprising dazzle of colors. Magdalena exclaimed something in Mayan, then translated her words to English. "It is a holy object."

"It is lovely," I said. "And it behaves like a prism, despite its unusual shape. I must say, I have never seen the likes of it." At that moment I had an intense desire to pick up the bird with my fingers and to examine it more closely, but I resisted. I did not want my companion to think I did not respect the dead, and besides that, I feared I might unwittingly damage it.

I used the remaining exposures for the birds, and then stored the camera and its precious film in my rucksack. After we had replaced the lid of the casket, we departed the crypt.

One at a time we squeezed through the partially open door, then donned our packs and climbed the stairs. As we approached the opening, I felt an immense sense of relief. Even if Valdez were to steal the contents, knowledge of them would not be lost to science.

"Now," I said to Magdalena as we exited the crack in the earth, "We need to conceal the entrance."

"And who would you be concealing it from?" said a deep male

voice. I had not noticed him in the blinding sunshine.

"Mr. Batista!" I cried. "You startled me!"

"Why?" He smiled, raising a dark eyebrow quizzically. "Are you up to something dishonest?"

"How dare you insinuate that!" Magdalena interjected.

"Then why the secrecy?" Professor Valdez walked up behind Batista, flanked by the baron and two young men, no doubt students. "As I told you, Batista, our young Miss D is cleverer than she seems. Under that brilliant intellect lies a cunning, conniving female soul."

"Thank you, Professor," I said. "If that was meant as a compliment."

"It was," the Professor said. "We greatly appreciate your finding this for us. Now I must insist, as administrator of this archaeological site, that we inspect your belongings."

"We are not thieves!" Magdalena snarled. "Go inside and see. We have taken nothing."

"Nothing personal, ladies, but I cannot take the chance. Your secretive behavior alone is sufficient grounds for suspicion. We must see your packs."

"You will find we have taken nothing," I said. Reluctantly we handed over our bags. Though we had nothing to fear, the invasion of our privacy was infuriating.

"Supervise the search, Mr. Batista," Valdez said. "The baron and I will check the interior." Valdez disappeared inside. The baron followed. Even holding his breath he could barely squeeze through the opening.

"Ladies," Batista said. "This is not my choice. Personally, I trust your word."

As he said this, the two students opened our packs and began placing the contents in two neat piles on the ground. The one who was checking my things examined my camera curiously, perhaps not recognizing what it was.

"No!" I cried. "Don't do that!"

It was too late. He had already opened the camera, exposing the film within.

"Luis! Apologize to the Señorita!" Batista demanded.

*"Perdoneme,"* he mumbled, blushing despite his dark complexion.

"Let me do this," Batista said, motioning for him to step aside. He picked up the leather roll that housed my collection of archaeological tools. "How fortunate you are, Miss D! Our students do not have access to this caliber of equipment."

"It was a gift from my father."

"Lucky girl." Batista winked. To the students, he said, "Now put everything back."

"I will do it," I said, snatching my pack from the boy.

Soon afterward, Valdez and von Tuntenhausen emerged from the opening. "What an astonishing find! The tomb of an unknown queen!"

"Is that so?" asked Batista, grinning at me. "You are a woman of many talents."

"Indeed she is. I thank you ladies for this most spectacular discovery. And now, I must insist you leave Tikal immediately."

"What? Why?" I gasped.

His formerly pleasant countenance was replaced by a harsh scowl. "You have disregarded my orders, gone exploring in a dangerous area and have entered the tomb without first obtaining my permission. I am especially disappointed in you, Señora Ruiz. I would not have expected Miss D's guardian to act so irresponsibly."

"That's not fair!" I cried. "You should blame me; I talked her into it."

"Miss Dfrdwy," Magdalena said, taking my arm, "The man is within his rights." To Valdez, she said. "We will respect your wishes and depart. However, it is now late afternoon. By the time we have packed our belongings, it will be dark."

"We must not to put the ladies in danger," said the Baron.

Valdez exhaled loudly, as if the very fact of our existence was exasperating. "Very well. You must leave by the morning. You will remain at your campsite until then."

"Professor Valdez," said Batista, "Surely the ladies didn't mean any harm. If there was nothing missing, and no damage to the tomb, doesn't that mean they can be trusted?"

"Batista!" snapped the Professor. "I am in charge here. It is not your place to decide. In any case, your judgment is suspect. It is obvious you are smitten with young Miss D."

The young man's mouth fell open. "Smitten? I merely endeavor to be a gentleman. My apologies, Professor, I did not mean to overstep my bounds." He did not meet my eyes as he spoke, which was just as well, because I was blushing with anger and embarrassment.

"*Merde!*" I muttered under my breath. It was a word from my mother's days as an actress, an uncouth word she never used except at the height of her anger. That was how I felt at the prospect of having my visit cut short. And how rude it was for Valdez to call attention to Batista's infatuation with me!

"Batista, escort the ladies back to their tent, and ensure that they remain there. Juan and Eduardo," he said to the students, "You will wait here and stand guard. Do not enter the tomb or disturb anything, or I will have your hides. I will have the Major send two soldiers to take your place as soon as possible.

Inside, I was seething as Batista escorted us back to our encampment. Valdez' accusations against us were preposterous. The Professor had never said I needed permission to explore, nor had he expressed any requirements about informing him. Worse yet, Father would be very disappointed with me.

As soon as we were back inside our tent, I turned to my companion and said, "Señora, why didn't you –"

She put a finger to her lips and led me away from the door as she continued with a whisper. "I am every bit as upset as you are. But you must not underestimate Professor Valdez. He is not a man to be trifled with. He wants us out of the way, and has given us a chance to depart peaceably. If we refuse, he may find a more brutal method."

I gasped. "He wouldn't dare! I cannot believe he would resort to violence."

"I sincerely hope not, but we cannot take that chance. These treasures, wonderful as they are, are not worth our lives." As I sat, dumbfounded, she continued. "While you were on your early morning exploration, I went to see Valdez to inquire whether he knew of your whereabouts. As I approached the work site, I heard him shouting like a madman. He was giving some poor student the most dreadful dressing-down. The young man's cheek was red, and not from embarrassment. I believe the Professor had struck him."

"Goodness, that's terrible. What could the poor boy have done to deserve such treatment?"

"I don't know, but Valdez told him to pack up his things and leave at once. Like us, he was to be banished from the site. Whether or not Valdez is dishonest is an open question. Nonetheless, we need to be wary of his temper."

Magdalena and I return to Tikal.

# VII. Desecration

That night, I lay awake on my sleeping mat, seething, as Magdalena snored quietly. I could not accept that my Mayan adventure was to be cut short. Shortly before dawn, I gave up on sleep and dressed quietly. Using one of father's wonderful gadgets, a bulb containing essence of firefly chemicals, I got dressed and wrote a quick note. "I'm sorry, but I must see something. Tell them I have taken ill and you don't wish to rouse me."

I was glad I had packed the special hunting outfit Mother had made for my excursions with Father. It was similar to my riding jacket and breeches, but covered with green and brownish blotches in a pattern the French call camouflage, which helps one hide from one's intended prey when in the forest. Though my mother had no desire to participate in such activities, which she considered barbarous, she was all too happy when we brought back wild game such as partridge and rabbit, which she and I would cook together.

As wonderful as the camouflage outfit was, it was not magic, and I had to travel off the path as silently as possible. Using my compass, I was able to locate the queen's tomb without becoming lost. As I approached I heard voices; even this early in the morning, the site was already abuzz with activity. I found a tree that I could climb for a better view.

I peered through my binoculars toward the tomb. Batista was at the center of the activity, directing the workers as they emerged from the crack in the earth with the tall, decorated clay pots. "Do not break anything, or there will be hell to pay," he said.

Something seemed to me to be amiss, and I realized that these were not students, but uniformed soldiers. Furthermore, unlike the operations the main excavation site, they were not documenting and recording the artifacts as they found them. They were simply packing them up and taking them away.

They were in such a hurry to remove everything from the tomb that I once again questioned the Professor's motivations. If their motives were purely scientific, they would have proceeded more cautiously, studying and cataloging each object. I lowered the telescopic lenses from the brim of my pith helmet (which I had attempted to disguise with leaves and splashes of mud) for a closer look at the scene. Batista was bent over a wooden box, which was filled with packing material, perhaps shredded paper. He appeared to be inspecting some smallish objects packed within; from my perch I saw a glint of gold and silver, as well as a splash of color. The bird figurines! Of course these would be the Professor's top priority.

I hurried back to camp, no longer so worried about discovery, though I quickly ducked into the brush when I heard voices approaching. There was smell of pipe tobacco, and I heard the Baron droning on about something, with the Professor walking beside him.

*It might all be innocent,* I reminded myself. The objects would need to be removed for study, and for safekeeping against looters. Remembering the Professor's outburst on the previous day, I became even more skeptical.

I managed to get back to camp without being detected.

Magdalena was preparing her automobile for the trip, filling the boiler with water and the firebox with wood. She did not greet me, but gave me an evil glance.

"I am sorry, Señora," I said. "But I needed to see what they were doing at the tomb we discovered."

"You were most reckless to act so irresponsibly," she began, "But I am happy that you've returned safe. Quickly, pack your things; we must depart. My village is not terribly far, but the road is not good, and I wish to get there before nightfall."

I did as she had requested, placed my bags in the boot of her vehicle, and then pulled out the stakes and turned the crank to fold the tent into its transportable form. I was glad I had not delayed further, because Valdez arrived to ensure we were leaving. Batista was at his side, of course, and he made a big show of bidding us farewell and kissing each of our hands before we climbed into the steam carriage.

Magdalena's village was to the north of Tikal, so we did not return the way we came. Rather, we continued along the trail through the ancient city. We passed a pair of bored-looking soldiers standing guard at another shack beside the road. These two woke up when they saw us and waved at us with big grins on their faces.

As I was looking back toward Tikal, I spotted something in the sky. "Another balloon!" I cried. "Could we stop, please?"

"Just a bit further," she said. "Where the guards can no longer see us." After we had rounded the corner she pulled the car to the side of the road and stopped. "Where is it?"

"There," I pointed. "The olive green dot, approaching from the east."

"Interesting," she said. "It is definitely not the supply balloon.

71

That only comes once a week, and to my knowledge, the only craft they employ is Señor Obregon's blue and white balloon."

"I wonder who's aboard." I jumped out of the car and grabbed my spyglass from the back. "Two men, in uniform," I said. "They are definitely not from the Guatemalan army. In fact, they look British."

"May I see?" Magdalena took the glass as I handed to her, and peered into the sky. "Yes, those certainly are English uniforms."

At the craft approached, it was losing altitude. I took the spyglass and climbed into a nearby tree as Magdalena shook her head at my impetuousness. I could see only for a moment before the balloon disappeared behind the forest, but I was certain they were landing near the work site. I returned to the ground, disappointed that I hadn't been able to see more.

"No wonder Valdez was so eager to send us on our way," I said.

"Why do you say that?"

"This would be the perfect route to smuggle out antiquities. Through the colonial garrison in British Honduras."

"Perhaps," Magdalena replied. "But wouldn't it arouse the suspicion of the students?"

I shrugged. "As you observed, Valdez rules them with an iron fist. Though Batista would almost certainly have to be part of the conspiracy."

We resumed our journey. Magdalena drove on in silence, and I sat beside her in silent contemplation. There was something amiss at Tikal; that much was certain. What was the extent of the conspiracy, and was there anything we could do to stop it?

# Miss Ione D. and the Mayan Marvel

Magdalena's home village was closer than I had anticipated. We arrived there before mid-afternoon. It was much like the place where we had stayed with her aunt, with small thatch-roofed stucco houses lining the main street. As we entered, a number of children stared and pointed. Many began to run alongside the car, laughing and shouting, so we had our own escort by the time we stopped.

The older children shouted greetings as we disembarked, mostly gathering around Magdalena, who smiled and answered them in Mayan. The building beside us was larger than the others, with a tile roof instead of thatch, and a cross on the top. A man in black robes came out of the entrance of the church and waved at us.

"Señora Ruiz," he said. I was glad to hear him speak Spanish, as my comprehension had increased considerably. "It is good to see you again. I am very sorry for your loss."

"Thank you, Padre," she said. "This is my traveling companion, Miss Ione. Her father works for the American Embassy in the capital."

"*Mucho gusto*," I said with a smile, then curtsied. I realized that my companion had not told me of the reason for her visit, save that it was "business" of some sort. I felt sad to learn that someone near to her had passed away.

We followed him through the church, a tiny place with whitewashed walls, wooden benches for pews, and a hand-carved, brightly painted crucifix behind the altar. Magdalena and the priest spoke too rapidly for me to comprehend, much as I tried to follow along. As we exited the church, we came to a small cemetery. We approached a grave that was adorned with a carved wooden cross. Unlike those on the neighboring plots, its wood looked fresh and unweathered.

"Eduardo was a good man," the priest said, "But with few friends and precious little family. Sister Annamaria was the only relative at the funeral. It is a shame you could not attend."

"My brother and I were estranged," she replied. "And his wife passed away long ago. We have little surviving family in this area."

"I visited him during the brief illness before his passing. He asked about you, and expressed his regret that he had kept you away."

"I am glad to hear he was thinking of me." Magdalena spoke without emotion in her voice, but I noticed that her eyes were glistening in the midday sun.

We bowed our heads as the priest prayed over the grave. It made me said to think that the poor man had died alone.

As I soon learned, Uncle Eduardo and his wife had no children, so he had left all his worldly possessions to his sister. Perhaps Magdalena's sister could not accept them, having taken vows of poverty.

As the town was quite small, we walked the short distance to Eduardo's home. Like those of his neighbors, it was quite modest. I was surprised to learn that the large open field behind it had also been Eduardo's. It was surrounded by a wood rail fence, and two horses grazed within.

"They're beautiful!" I exclaimed. There was an all-white mare and a sturdy gelding with a deep black coat.

"Yes," Magdalena said. "Our family was fortunate to have horses, as most people in this village could only afford a burro at most. I loved to go riding as a child."

"How wonderful!" I exclaimed. "Would it be possible for us to ride them?"

"I suppose so. Eduardo was not well in these last few months, so hopefully they have not gone wild. But first, we should eat. Kindly use this shovel to dig some yams from the garden."

The two of us prepared a simple but filling meal from the yams and some sugar and spices. Though at first I had missed my mother's cooking terribly, I was beginning to appreciate the cuisine of Guatemala. Someday, I reflected, I would like to tour the world and sample the fare of every nation.

Afterward, we went to the back of the house where the saddles and bridles were hanging. The horses did not protest being saddled, so it appeared that Eduardo had kept them in practice. Magdalena road the gelding, whose name was Hidalgo, and I the mare, which was called, appropriately enough, Fantasma.

"It is wonderful to be riding again," I said as we rode our mounts down the road. "I know that machines are the way of the future, but there is something about this communion with another living thing that the world will miss."

"Yes." She did not seem to be enjoying this outing as I was. Perhaps she had been too busy to mourning Eduardo's loss. Now, in her home village, I imagined the feelings would be more poignant.

"Would you like to talk about your brother?" I offered. "When my grandmother died last year, I was very sad, until my mother suggest I write down a story about her life, a sort of memorial and a celebration. Somehow that made me feel better."

Magdalena shook her head. "We were not close in recent years. I appreciate how he has left me this property, and I shall take a few mementos, but I cannot live here anymore. Perhaps I shall give the land to the nunnery where our sister dwells. They can use the money to help orphans like us."

"That would be a good thing." After a pause, I added, "Señora Magdalena, I am sorry to hear about your brother, but I am also sorry that my rash actions got us expelled from Tikal."

"No, I am not angry at you. I have been preoccupied about something about which I didn't tell you. Last night, as you were sleeping, I lay awake for some time. Finally, I dressed and left the tent. I meant to speak with Valdez, in an attempt to convince him to change his mind. He was not at his tent, but I heard loud voices coming from the mess tent. He and his companions were drinking and playing cards.

"This was good, I thought. I would catch Valdez in a celebratory mood. But then I heard the Baron complaining about losing too much of his money to Valdez. That was when Valdez responded, in German, 'You will earn enough from our new discovery that your losses will be but a drop in the ocean.'"

"At that point I returned to our tent, angrier than ever. I believe that half the night had passed before I was able to sleep."

"So we have more than evidence, we have proof! But why didn't you tell me this?"

"I did not want induce you to do anything reckless. As furious as I am about what Valdez is doing, I do not want to risk your safety, or mine. Confronting Valdez could be dangerous."

"Perhaps we need not confront him. If we tell my father he could use his influence with the President to spur the Guatemalan government to action."

She shrugged. "It would be our word against that of a man who has powerful friends. And even if the President did intervene, by that time, these treasures would be lost forever."

"Yes. If only that foolish boy hadn't exposed my film and ruined my pictures! With concrete physical evidence such as that, we could hold the Professor accountable." I jerked on my mount's reins to bring me closer to Magdalena. "We must return to the camp and see where he has hidden the things he has plundered from the queen's tomb."

"No! As I said, it would be too dangerous."

"Then I shall be forced to go there myself, even if I must walk the entire way."

"I cannot permit that."

"Señora, please. I must make this right. I cannot bear to think of how that... that blackguard Valdez may escape punishment for his crimes. Nor do I wish to see your peoples' heritage lost."

She nodded. "I understand. If I do not grant you permission, you would go anyway, wouldn't you? In that case, I shall accompany you there."

"No, honestly, I would not disobey you! But thank you, thank you so much for agreeing to go, Señora Magdalena! I promise that if we are caught, I will take full responsibility."

"I appreciate that, but being prosecuted for trespassing is the least of my worries."

I knew that, and felt a pang of guilt about exposing her to possible consequences, but was too excited to let that stand in my way. "We must leave at once." As I said this, the difficulty of the undertaking gave me a sick feeling in my stomach. "But how shall we get around the guard station? Surely the soldiers will know that Valdez has banned us."

"We shall go on horseback, and bypass the guard station. There is a stream that crosses the main road about half a mile before there. There is a trail that follows that stream, which will take us to Tikal, though by a more circuitous route."

"Good. The horses will be much quieter than the steam carriage, and hopefully they will be occupied with packing up their ill-gotten loot. If I wear my hunting outfit perhaps I could climb a tree and use my spyglass without being seen." I looked at Magdalena. "Do you have any similar clothing?"

"No, but I will look through my brother's work clothes, which are all quite drab in color. They will be much too large for me, but perhaps you can help me modify them to fit."

"Certainly," I said.

# Miss Ione D. and the Mayan Marvel

We witness an astounding illusion.

# VIII. Determination

We proceeded first to the site of the queen's tomb, which to my surprise was completely unguarded. "They must have removed everything of value," I said.

"Would you expect the Professor to do otherwise?" Magdalena asked.

We continued on to the main camp in a roundabout fashion, avoiding the well-traveled paths. It was slow going, since we had to find a way that was open enough for the horses to pass. As we got closer, I could hear the sounds of the men shouting and working at the excavation sites.

"Wait," I said. "I need to see if it's safe to proceed."

I dismounted from Fantasma and climbed up a nearby tree. This time Magdalena did not object, but I could tell from her expression that it made her uncomfortable.

From my perch I could see Valdez' personal tent. He, the Baron, and the Englishman were sitting in front of it on portable stools, engaged in an animated conversation. At one point, Valdez got up and disappeared into his tent. When he returned there was something golden in his hand. Was it one of the birds? It was too far away from me to tell. As I watched, Valdez pocketed the shiny object. Before departing with the Englishman, he said something to Batista, who remained at the entrance.

"How can we approach them without being seen?" I asked.

"There is no way," she said. "But perhaps you could more readily explain your presence if it appears you are here without my permission."

"That makes sense." I gave Fantasma a little kick and rode on toward the Professor's tent, while Magdalena followed some ways behind on Hidalgo. If I was caught, the worst Valdez could do would be to send me back to Guatemala City. As dishonest as he appeared to be, he would be too smart to harm me, thereby causing a diplomatic incident.

Batista was still by the Professor's tent, sitting on a stool and writing in a journal of some kind. I turned and signaled for Magdalena to join me.

"It appears," she whispered, "that your admirer is on guard duty. That would imply there is something important inside."

"I agree. But how can we get in?"

"As much as I hate to suggest this, you must distract him, either with conversation, or perhaps a request for his assistance. While you have thus occupied him, I will check the Professor's belongings."

"Yes!" I clapped a hand over my mouth, afraid Batista might have overheard. "That's a brilliant plan." Despite my excitement, deep down I was worried. I hated to be privy to something illegal. Even more so, I hated to involve

Magdalena.

I removed the camouflage jacket, so that it would not appear that I had been sneaking into their camp. He did not notice as I approached until I said, "Mr. Batista?"

"Miss D!" he cried. "What are you doing here?" He looked around, a stricken expression on his face. "The Professor will be furious if he sees you."

"My apologies for troubling you," I cooed. "I shall only be here for a moment, then I will depart." I then told him how I had lost the precious ivory comb my mother had given me, and I sincerely wanted to find it. That much was true, though I did not say that I had lost it the year prior in Coventry. "I have not seen it at our former campsite, and I would dearly like it back, for it belonged to my grandmother. Perhaps the assistance of another person could speed my task."

He glanced over his shoulder at the tent behind him. "This is most inconvenient, and highly irregular. I suppose I could assist you, at least for a few moments."

Holding the horse's reins in my hand, I waited for Batista to stand up and join me. "That is a fine animal," he said. "To whom does he belong?"

"To the family of Señora Ruiz. I borrowed him so I could come and search for the comb."

Batista eyed me suspiciously, but he did not inquire as to how I had gotten past the soldiers' checkpoint. As we walked down the path, he spied a dust-covered student returning from the dig.

"Raul!" he cried. "I need to see to some urgent business. Go sit in front of the Professor's tent until I return."

"Why?" asked the student. "I have finished my work for the day."

"Don't question me, just go!"

"Yes, Señor Batista." The student hurried to comply.

There were butterflies in my stomach. Would Magdalena have time to complete her mission?

Satisfied that the tent would be watched, Batista appeared to relax. We hurried to our former campsite and searched the ground around it quite thoroughly. Though of course we did not find the comb, we did find a tent stake I had neglected to pack with me.

"I am sorry, Miss Ione. I am quite certain your grandmother's comb is not here. You must go, before someone sees you here."

"That is unfortunate," I said. "Although I really appreciate your help." I turned to Fantasma, put my foot into the stirrup, and lifted myself onto her back. It was not a lady's saddle, but since I was wearing dungarees, I was able to ride astride, like a man. Batista must have found this shocking, because he stared at me for a moment, wide-eyed. "And now, sir, I must bid you adieu."

"Adios, Señorita." He stepped closer so he could take my hand and kiss it. "Perhaps I should escort you past the work site, to make sure there is no trouble."

"That will not be necessary," I said. "Again, thank you!" I took the reins and spurred the horse into action, sending him cantering through the trees, keeping my head down in case of low-hanging branches. If Batista felt inclined to follow me, he would not be able to keep up with us on foot.

I met Magdalena at the appointed meeting spot, which was along the stream we had followed to Tikal. She was sitting Indian-style, her back against the flat surface of a large rock, as Hidalgo ate the grass along the banks. Her face was flushed, and her always-neat hair was a mess.

"Were you able to find anything?" I asked her, as I swung my foot over the saddle and dismounted.

"I only had a moment to look." Magdalena stood up and approached me. "Before a student arrived to take Batista's place. But I did manage to find this." She pulled a small object from the pocket of her jacket, which sparkled in the half-light that filtered through the thick vegetation all around us.

"The crystal bird!" Thank goodness at least one had been saved. Though some might have preferred to rescue the gold or silver figurine, this one was, in my opinion, the most intriguing. "May I see it, please?"

She handed it to me, and I held the ancient object for the first time. It was smooth and cool to the touch. In order to see it better, I stepped into a place where the sun shone brightly through the trees. Since it was many times brighter than the lantern by which I had seen it before, the rainbow effect was proportionally more intense, a brilliant blaze of color.

"It is so beautiful." My voice dropped to a half-whisper, as I was in awe of the artifact. "Professor Morales will simply be thrilled to see this!"

"Indeed. Even so, it is a shame that the others will be..." She paused, a sudden look of terror on her face. "Do not move!" she said in a low voice. "Stand perfectly still!"

"What?" I followed her eyes to the rock where she had been sitting. There, crouching in front of it, was a jaguar, teeth bared, and tensed as if ready to pounce. The sight so startled me that I dropped the bird from my hand, whereupon the jaguar disappeared.

"Madre de Dios!" Magdalena exclaimed. "Where did it go?"

"I did not see where it went," I said. "It was there one moment, and then it was gone." I bent down to pick up the artifact. "I am grateful there was soft grass around my feet, and not rock, or this might have broken." I held it up in the sunlight to make sure the object was undamaged.

"There!" Magdalena pointed again. This time, we could see the image of the jaguar upon the flank of her horse, as if it were a very elaborate brand. The big cat remained still and flat as a painting, definitely not real in any way.

"This is astounding!" I said. I tilted the bird in my hand to view it more closely. As I did this, the jaguar image came to life, opening and closing its jaws and blinking its eyes.

"Is that an apparition?" my companion asked, her voice hushed with amazement.

"No, a projection. To me, it resembles one of Edison's

amazing motion pictures. Could the Mayans actually have invented such a thing, so many centuries ago?"

Magdalena nodded and smiled. "My people had many secrets that are lost to time, and have yet to be rediscovered."

I stuffed it into my vest pocket, wishing I had some cloth in which to wrap it. "We must leave immediately. Valdez will notice that this is gone."

We were about to mount our horses when we heard men shouting. Batista's voice rose above them. "I am certain that she went in this direction!"

"Quickly, we must hide!"

"But what about the horses?"

"We shall have to..."

"Aha, we have found the guilty parties!" Professor Valdez declared. "You must surrender what you stole!" He emerged from the woods, followed by a number of men: Batista, the Baron, the student Raul from before, the two men in English uniforms, and two Guatemalan soldiers bearing rifles.

"Stole?" Magdalena sneered. "Such impertinence! How dare you insinuate that I would profit from the heritage of my people!"

"Do not bother to deny your actions. One of the bird figurines is missing," said Valdez. "And young Raul observed you emerging from my tent, after your companion shamelessly lured Mr. Batista from his post."

I looked over at Batista, whose downcast eyes refused

to meet my gaze. No doubt he was in big trouble with the Professor, but I felt no guilt for my deception. It served him right, the scoundrel.

"There are strict laws against looting an archaeological site," Valdez continued. "Young lady, your connections may prevent me from prosecuting you, but I shall see to it that you and your family are expelled from this country. As for the nanny, well, you will be facing time in prison."

"I'm sure this all a misunderstanding is," the Baron said in his halting English. "Let us get from them the item and allow them to go on their way."

"Baron!" Valdez snapped. "Your position here is merely that of an observer. You are not in charge, and you will not tell me how to handle this situation."

The Baron's face reddened and he turned away, muttering in German. For the first time he seemed to be angry at the Professor's verbal abuse.

"What was that, Baron? If you have something to say, say it to my face!"

"Now, now, chaps, let's keep this civil," the Englishman interrupted. "Surely we can resolve this like reasonable men."

While this was happening, my mind was racing. How could we get ourselves out of this predicament? Of all the lessons I had learned from my parents, my professors, and my tutors, none seemed useful now.

Then an idea came to me. As Valdez and the Baron were arguing, I slipped the bird from my pocket and held it behind my back. Then I slowly stepped backwards toward a shaft of light that was breaking through the trees. Magdalena glanced at me and nodded slightly. As I felt the warmth of the sun hit my back, a flash of light issued from the crystal. A quick adjustment of my fingers caused the image to appear on the face of the rock, where it had been before.

"Jaguar!" Magdalena cried, pointing at the image.

One of the soldiers raised his rifle and fired. The echoing blast, followed by the zing of the bullet as it bounced off the rock, caused the men to stop in mid-argument and drop to the ground. In the midst of the shouting, screaming, and cursing, Magdalena grabbed my arm and we ran. I looked around frantically for Fantasma, but the loud noise had spooked her and caused her and Hidalgo to run off into the forest. Now we would be forced to flee on foot.

I followed my companion through the brush, my heart pounding and the crystal bird clutched tightly in my hand. What had I gotten myself into? How had I gotten mixed up in this sordid business? I had only wanted to see Tikal.

I was surprised that Magdalena could run so quickly, despite her short stature; she soon passed me and led the way through the trees. "When I was a child," she panted, "we would visit a cave in this area. This way!"

Under other circumstances I might have felt excited about exploring a cave, bats and spiders notwithstanding. Now, all I could think about was escaping Valdez, and protecting Magdalena's freedom and my father's career from the consequences of my actions.

Magdalena stopped so suddenly that I almost collided with her. Before us loomed a precipice and a drop of dozens of feet. As I dug in my heels, the rocks and dirt behind my boots were sent into the chasm below.

At the same time, my hand came open and the bird fell out. I could not see where it went, but it kept on falling until it disappeared with a splash below. Only a few inches beyond where we stood lay a pit that was partially filled with water.

"*Cenote!*" she exclaimed. "A sinkhole! Since I was last here, the cave has collapsed."

I looked down. The lake at the bottom of the depression, at least fifty feet below us, was surrounded on all sides with jagged rocks. The sides were steep, but there were tree roots poking through that could possibly serve as hand-holds. Perhaps we could hide beneath the overhang of the cliff on which we stood.

"Stop right there!" cried Professor Valdez from behind us.

*Miss Ione D. and the Mayan Marvel*

**Magdalena loses her footing.**

# IX. Dilemma

Valdez strode into the clearing, followed by his party. I looked down at the bottom of the sinkhole, briefly thinking of escaping by jumping into the water. But even if I could avoid the sharp rocks that surrounded the lake, I did not know what avenue of escape lay below. I might find myself trapped, and endangered not only by my pursuers, but by whatever creatures might be hiding there.

"Do not attempt to flee," the Professor continued, as if he had read my mind. "Your escape has been foiled by Nature herself. I advise you to step back from the brink, slowly. The ground around the edge of a *cenote* is not stable. It would be tragic," he sneered, "If you were to fall into the water and drown."

"If you had not taken off and run," said the Baron, "We might believe that story you told to Herr Batista. But by your flight you have your guilt admitted."

"Are you people all daft?" the Englishman interrupted. Though he spoke in English, it appeared he been following their conversation. "I don't care a rat's bollocks what these two have done and for what reason. What I want to know is," he looked directly at me, "How did you cause the apparition? Was it something to do with the missing artifact you stole?"

"Yes, of course, the artifact," Valdez said. "Hand it over, Miss D, or it shall only be worse for you. Even if your dear father can get you out of this scrape, he will not be able to save your nanny from prosecution. For God's sake, don't be foolish, girl. Give me the bird!"

"I do not have it!" I stammered. "When we came to the edge, it fell from my hands dropped into the hole!"

"Liar!" he thundered. As he advanced upon us, Magdalena and I instinctively took a step back. "Must I take it from you by force?"

At that very moment, the ground began to shake beneath our feet. I saw Magdalena's look of terror as a crack opened next to where she stood. I grabbed her hand, then fell to the ground as the dirt gave way beneath her, hitting the water with a loud splash.

My lower body remained on firm ground, but my head and shoulders extended over the precipice as Magdalena dangled below. It took all my strength to hold on to her hand as she hung there, panting like a cornered fox. Despite my efforts, I felt myself slipping on the rain-slicked grass. Frantically I tried to dig my feet into the ground. At the last moment, I managed to hook my boot around what felt like the root of a tree.

"Miss D!" Batista cried. I heard his footsteps approaching and prayed he meant to help us, rather than to finish us off.

"Stop right there, Antonio," Valdez snapped. "If these two meet their doom, our problems will disappear with them."

"Professor," Batista pleaded. "Surely you don't mean to let anyone come to harm. Especially in front of all these witnesses."

"Batista," the Professor rumbled. "Let me remind you of your participation in our endeavor. You cannot implicate me without incriminating yourself!"

Magdalena had been right. Professor Valdez was indeed a

desperate man.

"You cannot intimidate me," cried Batista. "I will not go to prison or hang for murder!"

As the two argued, I continued to try to regain my footing. Why was Batista not helping us? Why was he allowing the Professor to order him around?

"*Mira! El globo!*" shouted an unfamiliar voice, probably one of the soldiers. I recalled that the word meant 'balloon'. I didn't dare raise my head to look.

"The supply balloon? What in blazes is it doing here?" Valdez cried. "It is not due until next week! Batista, come along now. I will no longer tolerate your insubordination and interference!"

"But what about..." Batista interrupted.

"Shut up, fool! The women are done for. They will never survive the fall to the rocks below. Come along now, or suffer the consequences!"

As he said this, his voice grew further away, and I could hear the sound of running feet as the men departed.

Meanwhile, my arms burned with exertion, and inch by inch, I felt myself sliding toward the edge of the cliff.

"Miss Ione, let go of me, or you'll fall, too!" Magdalena cried.

"No! Hang on!" It was Batista's voice. "Baron, help Señora Ruiz, now!" I felt two strong hands grasp my feet and slowly pull me away from the brink. At the same time, the Baron threw himself on the ground and extended his arms, to grab Magdalena by her wrists. Though my muscles screamed for relief, I could scarcely force my hands to release her.

With a grunt of effort, Von Tuntenhausen lifted Magdalena and dragged her body to the surface. Fighting my exhaustion, I propped myself up with my elbows and looked back. "You may release my limbs now, Batista. Thank you."

Magdalena lay on the ground, panting. "And thank you, Baron. No, don't help me up; let me rest for a while."

"Yes," I said. Forcing myself to sit, I saw that Valdez and the others had left, and that only Batista and the Baron remained. I rushed to Magdalena to see if she was alright.

"Blazes, girl, you're bleeding!" Batista exclaimed. "Let me help you. Don't worry, the Baron will tend to Señora Ruiz."

"I looked down and saw a deep gash in my right arm, and dozens of bloody scratches on my left. Batista produced a handkerchief from his pocket and tied it around my arm.

Though I was immensely relieved that both of us were alive and unharmed, I was terrified of what would come of the whole affair. No doubt Professor Valdez would deny threatening us, and if the case went to court, it would be our word against his. Or would we even life to see that day? At present, we might be in as much danger as we were before.

As I sat there I heard a roaring sound like a burst of fire, from very close by, and a shadow fell over us. I looked up to see the familiar blue and white supply balloon landing right beside us. Squinting into the light of the setting sun, I could see that the basket held not one passenger, but three.

"Daddy!" I cried, fighting back tears.

## Miss Ione D. and the Mayan Marvel

I show the artifact to Father and Morales.

# X. Deliverance

My father jumped out of the basket before it had even touched the ground, and ran up to embrace me. "Ione! Thank God I've found you." He broke free from our hug when he saw Magdalena lying on the ground.

"Señora Ruiz! Are you alright?"

"Yes, though it was a close call," As she struggled to her feet, Batista extended a hand to help her.

I looked around and saw that the Baron had disappeared. Besides Magdalena and I, only Batista remained.

"Be careful," said Professor Morales as he disembarked from the balloon. "The ground near the edge is prone to collapse." He turned back to the pilot, who was attempting to hold the craft in place. "Fly the balloon to the usual landing place, and speak to the Major at once. Tell him that I want him to allow no one to leave the site."

I embraced my father once more and looked up into his eyes. "I'm so happy to see you, Daddy! I'm sorry, but there was trouble."

"We saw that from above," he said. "Why on earth was Professor Valdez brandishing a gun at this young man here?" Noticing my bandages, he added, "Goodness, Cabbage, are you hurt?"

"I'm fine, Daddy. But how did you know to come here?"

"Fathers have a sixth sense about things like that," he chuckled.

"The truth is, when I told Professor Morales about the contents of your letter, it was his sharp insight that led us to suspect something was wrong."

"But how? When I sent that letter, I knew nothing of the events to come."

"It was because of Señor Batista," said Professor Morales.

"Batista?" I exclaimed in surprise.

Batista said nothing. He looked downward and exhaled.

"Yes, Batista. He was one of my star students, until the unfortunate day I caught him cheating. He was expelled from the University and sent home to Mexico. When your father said you'd mentioned meeting him in your letter, I wondered if it was the same man. When I determined it was indeed him, I thought, why would Valdez employ someone who had left our institution in disgrace? Was it because he needed a confederate whose reputation was already compromised?"

"Daddy," I said. "You need to know that Mr. Batista saved our lives."

My father turned to the young man. "Then I owe you a debt of gratitude."

"Your daughter is an exceptional young lady," he said, as my father shook his hand.

"In that I agree with you," Morales responded. "Now, we must get to the bottom of this mess. Hopefully the Major will honor my request to keep everyone here."

"Now, Ione, will you tell us what is going on here?"

Father seldom called me by my real name, and when he did, it meant things were becoming quite serious. I told him all the things that had transpired since our arrival. I held nothing back, including my ascent of the Temple I pyramid and my unauthorized return to Tikal.

"Young lady, I should be angry with you for behaving so recklessly."

"But Daddy, I—"

"Wait, let me finish. I must also say that you displayed considerable bravery and cleverness in discovering what Valdez was doing."

"Thank you. And I'm sorry for acting so impulsively."

"More than impulsively—you have acted recklessly, pulled poor Mrs. Ruiz into your scheme, and have caused Professor Morales and me to leave the capital at an inopportune time. And look, you have torn your blouse. Your mother will be furious." Despite the severity of his words, as he finished scolding me there was a trace of a smile on his face.

"Yes, Daddy. I'm sorry."

"So now, what of this wondrous crystal bird you told me about? Where is it now?"

I sighed. "I lost it when Valdez and his men were chasing us. When they cornered us at the edge of the sinkhole, I was so frightened that I accidentally dropped it in." I pointed to the sunken lake below us.

Father approached cautiously and looked into the dark water. "Are you certain it fell down there?"

"I heard the splash as it hit the water. In addition, a piece of the cliff collapsed, and we nearly fell in. It's probably buried under a ton of rock and dirt now."

"If the artifact is as remarkable as Miss D says it is," said

Professor Morales, "We must find it. Tomorrow we shall dispatch a crew of students with shovels to dig until we find it."

"I agree," my father said. "By the way, Professor, did you bring a lantern?"

"Yes. I have a small one here in my pack." He withdrew the lantern, lit it, and shone it into the darkening pit.

"There!" I cried. "Something shiny on the cliff wall."

"By Jove, I see it!" Father exclaimed. "Professor, shall you and I go down and have a look?"

Morales shook his head. "It would be most difficult to descend safely."

"I will fetch some rope to aid you in your climb," Batista offered.

"No," said Professor Morales. "I will go get the rope, and you will climb down to get the artifact."

"Daddy, may I see the lantern?" I shone the light into the sinkhole once more. If the object we'd seen was actually the bird, it had not hit the water at all, but instead had lodged in the earthen wall near its base. Nearby in the water, a few feet from the shore, a huge mound of soil protruded from the surface. It was incredibly fortunate that this piece of the cliff had not covered or dislodged the artifact.

While we waited, Father used my spyglass to locate the best route to descend. Once Morales had returned with the rope, the men tied one end to a sturdy tree, and the other around Batista's waist. I started to say something to Father, but before I could speak, he said. "No, *mon petit chou*. The answer is no."

This prompted a puzzled look from Magdalena. "Why does your father call you a cabbage?"

I shrugged. It was my mother's expression, of course, and

sometimes there was no explaining the ways of the French.

We watched from above as Batista descended the rope into the sinkhole. I was quite jealous that Father had not allowed me to do it.

It took the better part of an hour for Batista to climb down, retrieve the artifact, rest for a while at the bottom, and then return to the surface. I realized that, though he might have gotten himself involved in dishonest dealings, there was also a heroic side to his character. He was as excited as a schoolboy when he returned, his face and clothes blackened with mud and the crystal bird in hand.

"My lady," he said as he handed it to me.

"Now," Father said. "Let us see this amazing bird."

I pulled a handkerchief from my pocket to wipe the bird clean and then held it up for them to see.

Father gave a whistle of appreciation. "It's beautiful, and considering the time it was made, certainly an accomplishment. But I'm afraid I don't know enough of Mayan culture to make a judgment."

"Allow me to have a look," Morales said. He took the bird from Father, and flipped down the magnifying lenses mounted atop his glasses to see it better. His eyes lit up with excitement as the last rays of the sun hit it, reflecting back a rainbow of color. He looked at Magdalena and me. "So this was with the queen in her tomb? I have never seen the likes of it!"

"It was hung from a cord around her neck," I replied. "There are four more, all of different materials. But this one is special. Hold it up to the sunlight, Professor."

Morales did so, and gasped as the jaguar image was projected across Batista's stomach, causing Father to laugh out loud.

"Astounding!" Morales cried. "As I have long theorized, the ancients had technology that we have yet to rediscover. So who has the remaining figurines?" he asked me. "Is Valdez in possession of them?"

"I hope so. It was why we felt we had no choice but to steal them back. We were afraid he would sell them to the Englishman, and we'd never see them again."

"Englishman?" asked Father. "This situation is becoming ever more complicated."

*Miss Ione D. and the Mayan Marvel*

At last, we see a real jaguar!

# XI. Deliberation

By the time we returned to the site of the main excavation, work had ceased, night had fallen, and the torches were lit all around. Major Garcia had convened a meeting in the mess tent, with about half the tables already occupied. Valdez sat at one, surrounded by four soldiers. Although he kept a smug expression on his face, I could tell by the way his eyes darted to and fro that he was desperate to escape.

Once again, neither the Baron nor the Englishman and his aide were present.

"My daughter has filled me in on what has happened," my father said. Since he was speaking Spanish, I was glad I was beginning to comprehend the language. "Now, we need to hear the other side of the story." He gave Professor Valdez a stern look.

"Thank you, Deputy Ambassador," said Major Garcia. "We value your advice in this matter, but there is a protocol we must adhere to." He eyed me suspiciously, as if wondering how much I had told Father.

"My apologies, Major," Father said. "Please proceed."

"We will entertain testimony from all the parties involved, beginning with Professor Valdez. Before we begin, I would like to remind everyone that this is an official proceeding and that lying will constitute perjury."

When called to testify, Valdez did not change his story. "This girl and her *babysitter* were caught breaking into a royal tomb."

"Is this true?" the Major asked me.

"We did not break in; the earthquake opened it. I merely wished to take photographs. Professor Valdez was the one who removed the artifacts from the Queen's coffin."

"You would have taken them, given the opportunity!" Valdez interjected. "Major, they entered my tent without permission, and stole one of the artifacts."

"Your Honor, I mean, sir," I said. "I believe that Valdez intends to sell them for profit."

"That is a serious accusation," the Major replied. "Pilfering antiquities is a criminal offense."

"As is perjury," snapped Valdez. "You know very well, sir, that we must remove these treasures in order to safeguard them from looters and treasure hunters."

"And what do you say, Señora Ruiz?" the Major asked. "Do you support the young lady's accusation?"

"I do," she replied. "Professor Valdez was speaking to an Englishman who arrived this morning in a hot air balloon," Magdalena said. "He showed him the golden bird. They appeared to be negotiating on its sale."

"That is a lie!" shouted Valdez.

I looked at Father, worried he might believe the Professor. To my intense relief, there was not disapproval but pride on his face. He was smiling just like he had on the day I had hit the bull's-eye on the archery range for the first time.

"So where is this golden bird?" the Major asked.

"It is in my quarters for safekeeping," said Valdez. "We were fortunate that these two," he indicated Magdalena and me, "did not steal that one, as they did the crystal bird."

"Crystal bird?" asked the Major. "Miss... D, do you have this in your possession?"

"I have it," Morales said. He removed it from his pocket, unwrapped it from the handkerchief, and handed it to the Major.

"And how did you come to have this, Professor?"

He explained how he had sent Batista down to recover the crystal bird from where it had lodged in the side of the sinkhole.

"Major, may I ask a question?"

"Yes, Miss D."

"What about the Baron von Tuntenhausen?" I asked. "He could confirm our story. And has anyone seen the Englishman?"

"I could not hold the Baron, due to diplomatic immunity," replied the Major. "As for an Englishman, I am not aware of any English visitors at this site."

I stared at him with narrowed eyes. Surely the arrival of the olive-green balloon could not have escaped his notice. If he felt the need to lie about that, most likely he had known of Valdez' activities all along.

"Professor Valdez," Major Garcia continued. "Do you have anything further to say?"

"Yes, Major. Although though I am completely innocent of all these allegations, I can no longer serve in this capacity under a cloud of suspicion. I hereby resign from my post with the University and will be leaving Tikal immediately."

"It is not up to me to accept your resignation," said the Major, looking at Morales. "As for leaving Tikal, I must insist that you remain here until we have investigated this matter further. Gonzalez, Paolo," he addressed two of the soldiers, "The Professor will remain in your custody until such time as we can bring him to the capital. Escheverria, search the Professor's belongings and confiscate any antiquities you find in his possession."

Valdez sprang from his seat, his face red with fury. "This is an outrage! Major, you of all people should realize the problems you are creating for yourself."

"Silence!" snapped the Major. "I do not appreciate threats. Now, as for you, Señor Batista..."

By this time, I was quite tired of questions and accusations. I also hated to see Batista punished, as much as he deserved it.

"Father," I whispered in his ear. "Señora Ruiz must find her runaway horses."

"Of course," Father nodded. "Major, may the ladies be excused? There is some urgent business they must attend to."

"Very well, but they must remain close by in case we have further questions. We will now take a fifteen-minute recess."

Father followed the two of us out of the tent.

"Sir," Magdalena said. "I wish to apologize for what happened, and for involving your daughter in this ugly business. I take full responsibility for what has happened. I shall be submitting my resignation from the Embassy."

"For what reason?" Father asked. "True, you were not quite successful in keeping my daughter out of trouble, but that is a tall order."

"Nevertheless, Mr. Dfrdwy," she said, her face impassive, "I was in charge."

"Daddy, no!" I cried. "It was all my doing! She did her best to stop me!"

"So you take full responsibility for this near-disaster? Your mother will be quite disappointed."

"I do," I said. "Send me to live with Grandpapa in France, or with Grandma and Grandpa in America, but do not punish Señora Magdalena."

"Now that you mention that," Father said, "I should hold you both accountable. You have gotten yourself ejected from the site, you have conspired to steal artifacts from their guardians, and you have almost gotten yourself killed." Despite his harsh words, he had the hint of a smile on his face. "However, I will overlook it this time."

"I appreciate your forbearance, Mr. Dfrdwy," Magdalena said, "But I still intend to resign."

"I won't hear of it! Now, you and my daughter must go find your horses before they are attacked and eaten by the jaguars everyone keeps talking about."

Providence must have smiled upon us once more, as we found the horses only a few hundred yards down the path. The two were grazing together in a clearing, as if the preceding fracas had never occurred. They did not try to flee as Magdalena and I each took one by the reins to bring them back to the main camp.

By this time, the meeting had adjourned. Father and Morales were standing outside the mess tent, talking and smoking cigars.

"Ah, here they are! I see you have found the horses," Father remarked.

"Yes," said Magdalena. "They are fine animals, and I would hate to lose them."

"You mentioned an Englishman," Professor Morales mused. "But no one seems to know his name."

"Sorry," I said. "All we know is that he arrived in a balloon coming from the east. We thought perhaps he was smuggling things through British Honduras."

"So what will happen to Valdez?" Father asked Morales.

"If what your daughter says is true," he glanced at me, "And I am inclined to believe her, then he will be tried and punished for his crime. Though of course it is possible there has been some misunderstanding. I promise that we will make a thorough investigation. Perhaps I shall remain here to make sure it remains fair."

"Will you require assistance?" Father asked. "Is the Major someone who should be in charge?"

I knew that Father, ever the diplomat, was really asking, could he be trusted?

"Unfortunately, there is no alternative at the moment, and I doubt he would recognize my authority, even though the University has jurisdiction over this place. If you could, please speak with the President about sending some of his forensic investigators."

"Of course." Father sighed. "What an unfortunate affair. So, Ione, this sordid business aside, have you enjoyed your visit here."

"Of course, Father. It was wonderful!"

"It is indeed an amazing place! I saw the pyramids as we flew over; it was as if Egypt had been transported here to the jungle. It is a shame that I must return to the capital tomorrow. Considering the circumstances, Kitten, I must insist you come with me."

"Yes, Daddy."

"And Señora Ruiz, you probably have not had sufficient time to resolve your family business. I will expect you back on the job by the beginning of next month, am I clear?" He betrayed his stern sounding words with a smile.

"Thank you, sir."

By this time, Garcia had ordered his soldiers to erect a pair of tents where we could spend the night. Despite my intention to discuss the day's events with Magdalena, I was asleep the moment I lay down on my sleeping mat.

The next morning we arose early and prepared to depart, but not before enjoying a hearty breakfast of eggs and ham prepared by Valdez' personal chef. The Professor himself, however, was nowhere to be seen.

"And now," Magdalena declared, "I must return to my village." Hidalgo was saddled up and ready to go, with Fantasma tied by her halter tied to the gelding's saddle.

I embraced my friend, tears forming in my eyes, even though I knew I would see her again in a few weeks' time.

"Take care, Miss Ione," she said. "You are a brave young woman. You remind me of myself at your age." I was surprised to see her eyes glistening as if she was holding back tears.

"Thank you, ma'am."

"Please, call me Magdalena. May you never give up your pursuit of knowledge."

"I won't."

She put her foot in the stirrup and swung into the saddle. "And beware of jaguars," she said in Spanish. "They come in all shapes and sizes."

"*Sí, voy a hacer eso.* And thank you for everything!" Father and I waved as she rode away.

"And now," Father said, "We must return home. Your mother has been so worried about you that she has scarcely been able to sleep."

"I feel terrible, but I wish she wouldn't fret about me! That is why I sent the note, and the wireless telegram."

"I know, my kitten. But you are her little girl, and of course she worries about you. We both do." He smiled and winked. "I know you wish to be treated as an adult, but in this case, it was for the best. If we'd thought all was well, I wouldn't have hired Señor Obregon and his balloon to come search for you."

After we bade farewell to Professor Morales, Father and I climbed into the balloon's basket. Once again it was raining, but all was dry in the shadow of the blue and white airbag. Señor Obregon stoked the fire of the burner, and we rose into the sky.

"So, Señorita," said Obregon. "When we last spoke, you told me you were on an adventure. Did it work out to your satisfaction?"

"It did, and it turned out to be more fascinating than I would have expected. I only have one regret."

"And what is that?"

"That I did not see an actual jaguar while here at Tikal."

Obregon laughed. "In my journeys, I have seen them many times. You simply need to know where to look."

"Cabbage, look!" Father cried. "In that tree!"

"A jaguar!" I gasped at its beauty. With its amber coat and dark spots, it was far lovelier than anything I had seen so far.

As fortunate as I had been in my life, to live in the great cities of

Paris and London, to see the beauties of Guatemala and explore the mysteries of the Maya, I knew in my heart that my adventures were just beginning.

Coming in 2017

## A new Ione D. Adventure!

*Professor Ione D*
And the Epicurean Incident

A STEAMPUNK TALE

*By* Treude & Holloway

Thanks to our cover models (left to right):
Arlys Endres as Ione, Anna Nguyen as Lily, Brittney Reed as Emma.

# Professor Ione D. & the Epicurean Incident
## A Steampunk Novella
by Vaughn Treude & Arlys-Allegra Holloway

## Chapter 1. The Epicurean Exhibition
### London, England, 1901

"There it is, up ahead, my good lady and gent!" proclaimed the driver in his charming Cockney accent. "The Crystal Palace!"

"Good gracious, it's monstrous," said O'Malley, my traveling companion.

"Monstrous? I find it beautiful." I put my notes aside, then leaned my head out the window of the horse-drawn taxi for a better look. For a moment, I thought the breeze might take my hat, but the weight of the apparatus concealed under the brim held it firmly on my head. I smiled in satisfaction as I withdrew into the passenger compartment. "Just look at it! Do you see how the setting sun shines on the glass?"

"I didn't mean to imply it was grotesque," my friend explained. "Rather, I didn't expect it to be so huge. Of course, to you, the world traveler, such wonders probably seem rather mundane."

"Not at all." I had to laugh at O'Malley's child-like jealousy. His new position at the *New York Sun* had afforded him little opportunity for travel. This was his first journey abroad in their employ. He had once been a war correspondent for the *Washington Post*, but the end of hostilities in Cuba had meant his reassignment to a tedious position as a copy editor. The *Sun* had rescued him from this purgatory by hiring him to write for their culinary section. Despite the fact that I had earlier applied for this same position, for which I felt I was better qualified that he, I bore him no ill will.

"What I meant was," O'Malley explained, "It's the first time 'cross the Atlantic for me. You, on the other hand, grew up here. So as I said, it would be old hat for you."

"I was only in England between the ages of ten and nineteen," I corrected him. "Still, it's wonderful to be back in London. The air is so much clearer now since they've made the switch from coal to fuel oil, so I shan't have the ghastly cough I had at the time. As for the Crystal Palace, I haven't seen it in many years, since my parents last brought me here as a child."

"I should have guessed you'd been here before," grinned O'Malley. "You were off seeing the world when I was sitting in a classroom, memorizing the Presidents of the United States, with my knuckles sore from Sister Agnes rapping them with a ruler."

"Well, since you're a few years older than me, I guess that means you were still making mischief in the upper grades."

"Who, me?" O'Malley laughed. "Perish the thought!"

O'Malley and I had both come from New York, though by separate conveyances, for the First Royal Epicurean Exhibition. Since his costs were covered by his employer, he had taken the luxurious – and expensive – trans-Atlantic Zeppelin *Lord Nelson*. Though I was an invited guest at the event, I still had to pay for my own passage and had taken a much longer journey by ship. My position at Margaret

# Professor Ione D. and the Epicurean Incident

Gallard College in Brooklyn was rewarding in many ways, but not in the financial sense.

The Exhibition, a festival of food and cooking, had been decreed by the recently crowned King Edward, to promote the growth of the restaurant industry and to bolster the reputation of English cuisine. This last item was of particular interest to me. My fascination with the nation and its food had led me to write a history of British cooking, purely for the love of the subject.

"Blimey, look at the line!" our driver exclaimed. The horse whinnied as we pulled up behind a rattling steam car. "Easy, old fellow! Everybody and his little brother must be here today." He turned his head back to address us. "Apologies, sir and madam, it may be a bit of a wait 'til you can disembark."

"It's quite alright, sir," I said. "Who can be in a hurry on such a lovely day?"

I took the opportunity to quickly review my notes one more time. Though it was a sunny day in London, the interior of the carriage was in deep shadow, making reading difficult. Luckily, I was well prepared. I reached under the brim of my hat and folded down a magnifying lens, which was surrounded by a glowing frame of tubular glass.

"My word, what is that?" asked my traveling companion. "Another of your father's inventions?"

"Yes," I replied, "Though I've made some adaptations and refinements of my own."

"How does it provide illumination, without any heat or flame?"

"Father found a way to synthesize the chemical from the posterior of a lightning bug. All it requires is periodic exposure to sunlight."

"How ingenious!"

"Thank you." I turned to my notes and commenced reading them over for the hundredth time. I was rather nervous about the upcoming event. I had been invited because of the popularity of my recent book, *The History of British Cooking.* In fact, I was to deliver the keynote address at the opening banquet. Not that I was averse to public speaking, but I would be addressing an assembly of the most honored and accomplished people in the culinary world.

"I was thinking back to when we first met," O'Malley said, startling me from my studies. "You're wearing the exact same hairstyle you were on that day. I recall that I made a remark about it, and you said something about it being Mayan. To this day, I find it quite fetching."

"Thank you," I said, not looking up from my papers. "Someday I shall teach you to duplicate it. Though I suppose your hair is not quite long enough."

"Then I shall stop getting haircuts," he laughed. "Though I'm not sure how it would go with the color of my hair. I expect it'd make me look like a wild Druidic chieftain."

"Indeed, you would be quite formidable, especially if you grew a beard to match."

I found it sweet that O'Malley had remembered, as I forgotten all about it myself. Then again, his sharp memory and keen eye for detail had helped make him a successful journalist at the age of twenty-six.

I thought back to the day when my family had arrived in Washington after spending a year in Guatemala. As it was several weeks before I could resume my studies, I occupied much of my time that summer at the Smithsonian Institution. Thomas O'Malley was then a tour guide at the Museum of Natural History. We became fast friends, and he was a regular visitor to my family's home in Georgetown.

"Are you still going over your speech?" O'Malley asked.

"I just want to make a good impression. This being a Royal Exhibition and all, one never knows who will be in attendance."

"Oh, you're not nervous, are you, Miss D?" O'Malley said with a grin. "I should think by this time you could deliver your speech backwards if you had a mind to. Don't worry, though, I'm sure the King will be quite impressed. If nothing else, he'll love your hair."

"That's good to hear," I said, returning to my speech, mouthing the words silently in an attempt to etch them in my memory.

Fate, however, was determined not to allow me to concentrate. From outside the carriage came the sound of voices shouting. For a moment I feared there was an altercation, but then I realized they were chanting in unison, "Home Rule for Ireland!"

"What's going on?" asked O'Malley. "I hadn't heard they were expecting any protests."

"Bloody Irish!" the cabbie grumbled. "I'd steer clear of those troublemakers if I was you. Hopefully, the constabulary will clear them out soon."

"They are citizens of the United Kingdom," said O'Malley. "Don't they deserve a chance to air their grievances?"

"If it were up to me," the driver said. "I'd ship the lot of them troublemakers back to their potato fields."

My friend opened his mouth as if to retort, but then closed it and shook his head.

I glanced through the open window at our driver. Could the man really be that dense? Though O'Malley didn't speak with any sort of brogue, I'd have thought his red hair and freckles would have been a dead giveaway.

Ever the reporter, O'Malley opened his satchel and retrieved his notebook. He stared out the window at the protesters with their hand-painted signs, furiously making notes in pencil. I found myself captivated by the intensity of his gaze. I had forgotten how blue his eyes were. As he began writing on a new page, the lead broke, and he looked away from the window.

At that moment, our eyes met. He gave me an enigmatic smile before digging out another pencil and resuming his writing. I returned to my work as well, feeling a warmth in my cheeks. I hoped I was not blushing.

It had been at least two years since I had last seen O'Malley, though we had corresponded the entire time. The memory of our courtship brought a touch of melancholy to my mood. At the time, I was certain he was about to propose marriage. Indeed, he spent several hours on the porch with my father one evening, sharing brandy and a conversation to which I was not privy. As I helped my mother clean up the supper dishes, she was all smiles, making remarks such as "Your father and I were married in June, but I think the autumn is also a very romantic season, no?"

Thomas said nothing about their discussion, nor would Father answer my questions about it. The very next day, however, my friend came to me with unexpected news. "I've been promoted to a full-time reporter!"

"How wonderful!" I cried. "I suppose you shall be obliged to give up your part-time work at the Smithsonian."

"Of course. And that's not all! They're sending me to Havana, to report on the troubles down in Cuba. Some say America may even become involved in the war!"

"That is such a splendid opportunity! I wish I could go as well; it all sounds very exciting."

He'd laughed at my naiveté. "I know you love adventure, and I shall miss you terribly, but I'm glad you're not going because I couldn't bear the thought of you being put in danger."

"What about you? Won't you be in danger as well?"

He'd laughed. "If I can survive being the youngest of twelve brothers and sisters, I can survive anything!"

In the end, Thomas never did propose to me, which was somewhat of a disappointment but also a great relief that I would not be obliged to tell him no. Though he is a wonderful man, and I have always found the idea of marriage and a family appealing, I simply was not ready. I had one more year of college to finish my degree, after which I had hoped to travel and see the world, with no husband to tell me which places were "too dangerous for a woman."

The clip-clopping of the horses' feet ceased, bringing me back to the present and the carriage to a halt. O'Malley sprang from his seat and bounded out of the door, where he stood, holding it open for me.

I sighed; upset that I had yet to put away my notes. When I reached under the seat for my handbag, my hat, weighed down by the light-and-magnifier apparatus, slipped off my head and slid under the bench across from me. I was forced to bend down low to retrieve it as O'Malley waited, an amused smile on his face. Once I had done so, I quickly folded my notes and stashed them in my handbag.

In the meantime, our driver had gone around back to retrieve the valise containing my books from the back of the carriage and stood next to O'Malley waiting for his payment. Over the chanting of the men and ladies on the nearby walkway, I distinctly heard him muttering, "Dad-blasted Irish." He turned to my friend and said, "That'll be two shillings, please."

O'Malley paid him. I noticed that, despite my friend's obvious disgust with the man's remarks, he threw in a few pence as a tip.

I stood up quickly in an effort to disembark while O'Malley was thus occupied, but I was too late. He was back at the carriage door in a flash, and he took a hold of my hand to help me step down.

In my frustration, I stopped there and said, "That's so very sweet of you, Mr. O'Malley, but I am quite capable."

"Please, call me Tom. We have known each other for enough years that it would certainly not be improper."

"Yes, O'Malley," I replied in exasperation. "I don't know why you men persist in thinking we women are fragile. After all, I climbed the temple pyramids..." As I said those words, my foot slipped on the step of the carriage and I fell forward toward him. He put both his hands on my arms to catch me; his grip was firm and yet gentle. Somehow my face stopped just inches from his.

We stood there for a long moment, staring into each other's eyes. It was if we had never been separated. Then, just as I thought he might be about to act on some wild impulse to kiss me, there came the sound of shouting.

"Watch out! Runaway car!"

With his two strong arms, O'Malley thrust me back into the

carriage. My handbag flew from my hand and I landed on my back between the two seats. I looked up quickly and saw a crowd of people closing around the carriage, but my friend was nowhere to be seen.

"O'Malley!" I cried. "Tom, are you alright?"

# About the Authors

Vaughn Treude grew up on a family farm in North Dakota. The remoteness of his home, with few children his age nearby, made science fiction and fantasy a welcome escape. His favorite writers were Isaac Asimov, Robert Heinlein, and JRR Tolkien. He always planned to become a sci-fi writer, but the demands of life kept his various projects from completion. After several years as a software consultant, he realized that the same kind of discipline required for writing code could be applied to creating fictional worlds. His published works include the novels *Centrifugal Force,* a political thriller and *Fidelio's Automata,* a steampunk adventure involving mechanical spiders. He is the co-creator of the musical comedy *One Good Man* with Arlys Holloway.

Arlys Holloway grew up in Phoenix at a time when the city still had a small-town western feel. Her family raised goats and chickens in their back yard. She comes from a long line of women named Arlys, as are both her mother and daughter. She traces the name to a great aunt who was a noted opera singer. She has worked in an amazing variety of occupations, including a fourteen-year stint running her own day care business. After her divorce she spent several years in the on-line dating world. Her humorous (in retrospect) experiences form the basis of the play One Good Man, which she co-wrote with Vaughn Treude.

# Also from Nakota Publishing:

**Centrifugal Force** by Vaughn Treude

In this novel of a probable near future, America is sliding ever further towards tyranny. Dissident blogger Joel Walter is wanted for a crime he didn't commit. His computer-hacker friend Nephi introduces him to an underworld where technology is Americans' last bastion of freedom and privacy. Despite pervasive surveillance, Joel decides to assume a new identity and disappear into the technological underground. Ever-increasing repression drives Joel, Nephi, and others into open rebellion in a desperate bid to retain their precious liberties.

**Fidelio's Automata** an Adventure in Alternate History
by Vaughn Treude

*A stolen invention threatens his dreams.* Fidelio Espinoza, a brilliant and idealistic young Cuban, arrives in early 1900's America with the goal of perfecting his automaton, a machine that will free humans from the dangerous, backbreaking work of mines and factories. Here he meets Hank, a cowboy turned Quaker who has vowed to atone for his sinful past. After a prototype of Fidelio's creation falls into the wrong hands, the two men join forces with Nikola Tesla to prevent this creation from being used in the service of oppression.

## Short works by Vaughn Treude, now available on Amazon:

"Found Pet" – a down-on-his-luck salesman adopts a strange furry animal that has a mysterious effect on the people around him.

"Fidelio's Dilemma" – young Fidelio Espinoza must decide whether to accept the respectable job arranged by his father, or to follow his dream of becoming an inventor.

Stories by Treude appear in the following Flash fiction collections by George Donnelly, available on Amazon.com:

*Valiant, He Endured: 17 Sci-Fi Myths of Insolent Grit*

*Christmas in Love*

www.ingramcontent.com/pod-product-compliance
Lightning Source LLC
Chambersburg PA
CBHW060633130626
46555CB00002B/784